The Heart Short Stories

A Collection of Steamy Romantic Short Stories

Book 1: With All of My Heart

 By Olive Youngly

Book 2: The Damaged Heart

 By Olive Youngly

Book 3: Cougar's In Heat

 By Freda Bachmeier

Book 4: A Promise of Love

 By Anya Smith

Contents

Book 1: With All of My Heart by Olive Youngly 1

Book 2: The Damaged Heart by Olive Youngly 13

Book 3: Cougar's In Heat by Freda Bachmeier 27

    A Cougar In The Wild 29

    My New Boy Toy 38

Book 4: A Promise of Love by Anya Smith 47

    The Broken Promise 49

    A Very Long Day And Night 53

    Life's Twists And Turns 57

    And Now The End Is Near 62

Other Books by Olive Youngly 67

Book 1

There was a knock. Allison opened the front door without a second thought.

He stood in front of her in old, tattered clothes. His jeans were torn in several places and frayed on the bottoms. There was also an unmistakable caking of dirt on each piece of clothing. He had a pale face and a light beard that freckled his chin. She did not recognize him in the slightest, until Ali felt herself drawn to his eyes. They were the most beautiful colour of green that she had ever seen in her life. They were soft, expressive and sparkled when he saw her. A smile crossed his face that immediately reached his eyes.

The recognition then hit.

"Ethan," she whispered.

The man lowered his gaze for just a second. He seemed to shrink in height a bit, back bowed. Forcefully, he looked back up at her. Those beautiful green eyes were full of an almost forlorn sadness.

"Hi Ali," he said sweetly. Her ex-boyfriend from so many years ago was regarding her as though she was the most beautiful woman that he'd ever seen. He kept looking her up and down and then looking away, as if embarrassed.

It had been ten years or more since she'd last seen him. Yes, they had broken up when she was only nineteen years old, so it was probably close to ten years on the dot. They were barely in college! Still, this wasn't the Ethan she had dated when she was nineteen, not by a long shot. What on earth had happened to him? Between the tattered clothes, the unkempt facial hair and the sad eyes, he looked a total mess! She felt almost disgusted by his appearance and then subsequently disgusted at herself. Had she really risen so far that a dirty, messed up looking man disgusted her?

"What are you doing here?" she blurted out, before realizing how rude her words came across. "I mean...it's been like ten years and I barely recognized you at first. I'm sorry Ethan. You startled me, just a little bit."

"I know how I look," he admitted bluntly. A faint redness crossed over his pale cheeks that not even the shabby beard could hide. He ran a hand through his hair. It was still the same sandy brown color that Allison remembered, but it was much longer. He looked as though he was in dire need of a haircut.

"I fell onto some very hard times. It took a lot out of me. I'm sorry if I...if my appearance is somehow offensive."

It was Allison's turn to blush. She felt the heat rise in her cheeks. She hoped he didn't see her disgust, but she knew he did. How humiliating! How utterly humiliating!

"No," she said, turning her head slightly away. "I didn't mean to stare. It's not that you look bad, Ethan; it's just that you look nothing like I remember you. I'm sorry if it comes across at all offensively. I didn't mean to..."

Ethan took a step forward and looked behind her into the house.

"Oh come in," she motioned, leading him into the house and closing the door behind him. She was not usually so uncomfortable, so awkward, but his appearance had rocked her just a bit. She remembered too well the days that she had promised this man forever. She had promised him that she loved him with all of her heart and that they always would be. Now, well, they seemed to live on opposite ends of the universe.

Allison watched as Ethan's eyes scanned the house. They flitted from elaborate decoration to beautiful furnishing and that caused a little more heat in her cheeks. Being a moderately successful actress, she honestly had the opposite of hard times. Life had been kind to her and although she did not show her wealth in extravagant ways all the time, just by looking at her house, it was obvious what she had. She was never ashamed of her affluence, but it was hard not to when someone she loved had obviously suffered.

"Thank you," she murmured, not sure what else to say to his compliment. She carefully led him to the living room, feeling that it was modest, despite the house's size. She walked over to the couch and gestured for him to sit down. He did, immediately. "Can I get you a drink?"

He was still looking around the house, although she could see him trying not to. His eyes darted about and then went back to the ground. "No, thank you," he replied.

At his decline, Allison sat down beside him. She left a good foot of space between the two of them, not wanting to be too close to him. She tried to speak, but found her words came out dry. She was just so intimidated by the sight of him.

"It's been so long," she nearly whispered. It really had been years. There had been so much that had changed since the last time they had exchanged heartfelt declarations of love. Oh, nineteen year olds were way too quick to throw those into the air. "H-how have you been?" she asked, even though she knew the answer would not be a positive one.

Ethan laughed, faintly. It brought that smile back to his face. She had always been in love with his smile.

"About as good as I look," he admitted. "I thought things were going to start getting better for me, but honestly they've sucked. I've been living with friends, but those friends got into some trouble and after that I started living in my car. I...I need a favor, Ali, and I hate to ask it."

"Yes?" she asked. She was reluctant to ask, knowing that this was going to make them close again and not feeling entirely prepared for that. She also had a feeling she knew what he was going to ask and she could not deny him.

"I need a place to stay," he confessed. "I just need a room for a few weeks, because I have a job now and it's...starting to go my way. I wouldn't have asked you, of all people, but I've run out of halfway decent friends and well, everyone knew how well you were doing."

Even though she'd known he was going to ask, she still felt a heat cross her face. It was kind of hard to think about him staying with her, but she was more than willing to help him out. He was more than a friend. He was a man that she had given her heart to at one point in her life. She was not going to take that lightly and she was going to help him.

"Yes, of course," she murmured. "I have an extra room and you can stay as long as you need to."

Ali did not have much time to think of her houseguest at first. She had made her name as an actress, after all, mostly in television. She had a major part when she was in her early twenties, and even though she was no longer in a main role, she had a supporting role in a sitcom. She was reading through a very important script at the studio, one that could make her character quite popular. It was important to her, so she just pretty much trusted Ethan to not get into any trouble.

After a very long night at the studio, Allison came running down the stairs with a sort of bounce to her step. Her heart was pounding and yes, she felt like giggling. It was just so good. At the last rehearsal, she had been told that her character was so very popular with the fans that there was a chance she could be bumped to regular before next season. It would be as good as her major role five years earlier had been. Despite the stresses, Allison really loved being an actress. She felt that she was talented and deserved a little more credit. Things would be good.

She bounded down the stairs and right into Ethan. She went tumbling, but Ethan caught her instinctively in his arms. His arms were firm, holding onto her and not letting go until she found her balance. He laughed, a delicate but sweet laugh.

"Why hello there Ali," he said, smiling again. She realized then that he had shaved. His hair was still long but the thin beard was no longer there. He looked cleaner, his skin shining. He still wore old clothing, but the clothes were now clean. Allison's heart pounded in her chest as she was reminded of *everything* about him. Oh god, she had loved him when she was young.

"Hi," she responded, looking down at his chest. He then realized that he was still holding on to her and let her go, his face absolutely sheepish. "How are you doing Ethan?" she asked, trying to break the awkwardness that had frozen in the air between them.

"I am pretty good," Ethan said honestly. He looked down at the ground. "I can't thank you enough for this Allison," he said. "I know that our breakup wasn't on the best of terms and I didn't want to ask you, but...I can afford an apartment before the month's end at this rate. I cleaned up and...Yeah, the job is going well. I can't thank you enough."

"Oh, well, it's no problem," she said, running a hand through her hair.

He stuck his hands in his pockets. "So, what has made the lovely Allison so happy?" he asked. "I noticed the way that you nearly leapt into my arms..."

"I didn't..." she exclaimed, then started blushing and stopped when she realized that he was being playful with her.

"It's okay," he teased lightly. Even though he'd let go of her, Ethan's lips were only a few inches away from her. It felt strange and made her blush heavily. She had loved him so much when she was a teenager. She had to admit that their breakup was entirely her own fault. She had been self-centred and extremely focused only on herself and her own career. Not that she isolated him, or anything like that, but she had always been so selfish and demanding. She'd also pressured him in many ways. She was a crappy girlfriend. Now, she liked to hope that as a grown woman she was much more considerate. No, she couldn't think like that. She shook her head at the thought.

"Have you seen my recurring role on South High?" she asked. She didn't know if he followed her career enough, aside from knowing that she was a semi-famous television star.

"Yes, of course I have," he said. "Well, I'm not up to date, but I've seen Clarissa, your character. She's very cute. Of course, she is played by you."

Allison flushed. "People really like her," she admitted. "We're having an episode in a few months that's going to...maybe cement her as a more permanent fixture."

"Oh congratulations," he smiled, his eyes widening again. "I never really got to tell you, considering we broke up before you had your big break, but you're truly talented. You're...very good at making people laugh, but also portraying sitcom characters in a way that makes people think. I like that a lot."

"Thanks," she said sheepishly. "So where is this job you were telling me about?"

"It's at a magazine office," he said. "I'm basically everyone's assistant, but it's a good thing to be employed. Maybe I'll hit my break too."

"As a journalist..." she mumbled. She had never really fostered her boyfriend's dreams in the same way that he did hers. "That'd be great."

"Yeah..."

There was a long moment where they just looked into each other's eyes. Allison appreciated all of the sweet memories that passed through her mind, just from looking into his eyes. She loved her ex-boyfriend so much when they were together. She appreciated him in ways that she never could when she was a selfish teenager. She took a tiny step forward and somehow he bridged the rest of the gap. Their lips were touching and there was nothing she could do apart from lean forward and press her lips back to his, kissing him passionately. His tongue traced over her lower lip, but other than that, the kiss was kept absolutely innocent and tender. When she pulled back, her eyes were wide.

Ethan's eyes were dilated too and he looked terrified. His jaw hung low and his wide eyes kept avoiding hers. He was flushed red, cheeks a pink colour.

"Sorry," Ethan blurted out. He stepped back timidly. "I didn't mean to. I don't want you to think of me that way. I'm not taking advantage of you."

"No, of course you're not," Allison replied. She stepped forward and put her hand on his shoulder. "I missed you Ethan. I'm really sorry, you know?... For everything in the past." She blushed a little more as she remembered how she had treated him. She was glad that he still had feelings for her, at least some kind of feelings. She did not believe she deserved them.

Ethan looked up. Finally, his eyes met hers and he raised his eyebrows curiously. "Why are you sorry?" he asked.

"I was a terrible girlfriend," she lamented. She shook her head as the memories assaulted her. "I was selfish, didn't think about your needs nearly enough and still I was swearing up and down that I loved you. I was so immature."

Ethan smiled at that. It was a small, still timid expression that barely upturned his lips. "Sweetie," he said softly. He put a hand on her shoulder and Allison found herself once again getting lost in his eyes. "I think you forgot one major detail about that. We were only nineteen. We both were kind of... not so great at life, to put it lightly. It was over a decade now and I feel like we're a man and a woman, instead of kids. I still...feel something."

Ethan leaned down and kissed her again. It was sweet, gentle and barely a brush of lips at first. Her face reddened at the intensity of such a simple and innocent kiss. Allison found herself touching his face, fingers brushing over the freshly shaven skin of his jaw. She ran her fingers lightly over the skin, just enjoying the feeling of touch.

"I missed you," she whispered, pulling back from his kiss just so she could look into his eyes. Now, it wasn't that Allison had been pining for this man for the last decade; although the thought had often crossed her mind. She occasionally had that longing - the thought that maybe one day she could find her first love again.

"I missed you too," he stated. "I always wanted to seek you out, before things got bad, but I was too afraid. I just wish I could have come to you...better."

"You are amazing," he smiled and shook his head.

As they kissed, Allison forgot everything. She forgot about work, forgot about the world around her and forgot about the strange circumstances which brought Ethan to her doorstep. She carefully deepened the kiss, after making sure that it was okay with Ethan. He followed suit by tilting her head back and kissing her exploringly. They kissed as if they'd die without it. Allison supposed that those ten or so years led to a little bit of urgency. She tasted every inch of him in that kiss. She pressed her body close to his and she could feel that he desired her. They'd had sex when they were young, yes, but they had never really made perfect love. Instinct told her that they could now, if they both were willing.

"Can we go to my room?" she asked him, somewhat shyly.

Ethan nodded. A smile crossed his face that was so much bigger than the tentative one he'd given her before. He had a bright, energetic smile. Allison quickly shut the open window and made sure that the door was locked. She then rejoined Ethan. She took him by the hand and led him up the stairs. Her room was the farthest one down the hall. She opened the closed door and rushed in ahead of him, giggling playfully.

She hit the bed first. She bounced lightly and crawled backwards on it, beckoning him to her with a finger. He crawled up to her and then their lips were touching again. He kissed her and she kissed him back eagerly. She told herself that she was making up for so much lost time. She groaned deeply, amazed that she had this amazing feeling pulsating through her whole body. Ethan cupped the side of her face and stroked her skin lightly. His hand lingered under her blouse, cupping her breast. She let out a quiet moan, surprised at the intensity of such a simple touch. Then she encouraged him to take off her shirt and threw it aside.

Allison then rolled so that she was on top of him, straddling his hips.

"I've missed you so much Ethan," she said as she took off his shirt, lifting it over her head. Ethan had been a skinny young lad when they'd last been together, but the decade of absence had definitely given him a more toned, sculpted body. Having removed his shirt, she then raked her finger nails over the firm muscle of his chest and his abs.

They both removed the rest of their clothes frantically. Ali had to admit that even though they were adults now, they were still like teenagers in that aspect. Ethan looked at her with wide, adoring eyes.

"Ali, I meant this ten years ago and I mean it now," he gasped desperately. "You are the most beautiful woman I have ever seen in my entire life." Years of experience had taught Allison to determine the truth behind someone's words and she knew the man beneath her was being one hundred percent genuine about how he felt.

"You're sweet," she said, groaning as she realized how much desire she felt for him. She was burning hot and felt over-heated her at her very core. She stripped off her panties, returning back to the top of him.

He was obviously just as overcome as she was. Ali blushed at the feel of his need against her leg. It was not because she didn't share the need, of course. It was just because she knew that it was so mutual now.

She took him out of his boxers, stroking him adoringly. When she finally moved it was the best feeling in the world. She plunged down on top of him, filled so completely by the man she had once loved so much. Allison had total control at first, her hands on his hips. She controlled the speed and the depth of the thrusts, groaning at the feel of sweaty skin slapping lightly against her own sweaty skin. He looked up at her as though she were a goddess, hands sliding over her shoulders, down to her chest. He unhooked her bra, which she'd still left on.

Ethan turned the tables halfway through, as the arousal made Allison stutter in her rhythm. He flipped them around so that he was on top of her, lifting her legs up around his back so that each individual thrust of his hips drove her closer and closer to orgasm. He stroked her cheek, kissing her hungrily as he moved.

"I love you Ali," he grunted against her lips. "I've always loved you Ali."

It was something she'd never experienced before. Orgasm hit her like a wave at nearly the same time that she felt it hit her partner. She exploded on the inside in a rush of heat, squeezing her legs tightly around him and staring into his beautiful eyes. She felt him let go and heard his desperate moans. He seemed to moan over and over again. "God...good...God Allison..." he grunted out loud as he rode through the final waves.

When Allison came down from the rush of heat and the miniature rushes that followed, she leaned down against his chest. All she could hear in those blissful moments was the steady thumping of her lover's heart. She closed her eyes and seemed to drift off into a dream world. It was perfect bliss, at its core.

After her first night with Ethan, everything was a bit of a blur. Allison was still a busy woman and had to spend most of the next two days on set. The third day, however, her co-star Callista walked up to her and screwed up her face in disgust. Callista was, to Allison, a bit of a diva.

"Please tell me that you didn't screw your homeless ex," she laughed. When Allison didn't respond, still staring at her in slight shock, Callista thrust a tabloid newspaper at her. "I'd dismiss it as usual rag nonsense, but it was written by Ken Slater. He's always lurking around these parts and he's got a grainy picture that is so your house."

Allison looked at the tabloid article with horror on her face. Above it was indeed a grainy picture of her and Ethan, locked in their first kiss. It was obviously taken from outside her open window. The article headline simply read:

Sitcom Star Taken Advantage of by Scumbag Ex.

Regretfully, Allison read the article, if it could even be called that. It seemed to Allison to be two paragraphs of utter lies about Ethan.

Sources report that Ethan Thomas, an ex-boyfriend of sitcom star Allison Jennings has returned to her life. Thomas, a known convict, is known to be sleeping and lodging at Jennings California home. Former friends of Thomas indicate that he was arrested on drug charges last year and "will use Jennings for all she's worth." Photographs taken just outside of Jennings home that reveal the pair locked in an embrace.

"I'm worried for her," says an anonymous source. "She seems like a sweet girl, but Ethan's a con man. He'll play her good."

"This is utter stupidity," Allison cried out, because it was the first thing that came to her mind. She glared at Callista. The blonde was crossing her arms and staring at Allison as though the words of the tabloid were absolute gospel. Callista's eyes appeared wide and full of *concern*. Allison knew that even the concern was fake.

"Ethan is back in my life, yes, and he is an ex-boyfriend. This whole report is absolute idiocy though. Ethan is a good man."

"How long ago was it when you last dated him?" Callista asked innocently.

"Ten years ago," Allison murmured, knowing that for her idiot friend she was proving a point. She brushed right past her, walking back to the dressing room. She needed a moment of peace and she knew a scene was being filmed that had everyone else's attention. She needed to think about what she was reading for just a moment.

She looked at the article again. She had to admit one thing. Of all the journalists who wrote celebrity gossip, Ken Slater usually had pretty good sources. Allison's stomach dropped. She had not seen Ethan in ten years. Maybe the man was nothing like she believed him to be. Perhaps he had slept with her again to use her. What if he had a drug problem? Could he be at her house stealing even as she sat there! Panic overtook Allison who immediately stood up and looked around.

She wasn't alone. A young man with sandy brown hair was standing in front of her. He had a headset in his ear, but it was not turned on. She recognized him as one of the Production Assistants. His name was Matt, she thought.

"Hello?" she asked him, wondering what he was doing standing in the middle of the dressing room.

"Allison," he said softly, with a light smile and bright eyes. "I heard you talking to Miss James, erm, Callista I mean."

"Oh yes?" she asked defensively, standing up and crossing both her arms.

"I heard the rumours about your ex-boyfriend too," the Matt murmured. "I also know a way you can verify what's going on."

Allison turned to face him. "How?" she asked, trying but failing to hide the desperation she felt.

The boy brushed his hair back and a grin crossed his face.

"I'm not the only member of my family to be working a lowly job in the entertainment industry," he said with a slight laugh. "My sister is an intern at *Interest,* which you may notice is the trashy magazine that Slater works for. She was in the office when he came back with pictures of you and his story. She heard his source's name loud and clear."

"Who is it?" Allison blurted out.

"Janine Jankowski," the assistant responded with a wry smile. "Not exactly a difficult name to look up."

Impulsively, Allison leaned forward and hugged him. A blush crossed his face and he hugged her back, arms firm around her shoulders.

"Oh, but won't your sister get into trouble if it comes back around to Slater that I contacted his source?" she asked. As much as she detested tabloids and paparazzi, she wanted to let the poor lowly intern keep her job. She'd started from the bottom too and knew how much it sucked.

"She's leaving her job next week," the boy said happily. "She's got a better one and it was she who told me to tell you. She's a big fan of yours."

"Thank you!" Allison nodded, kissing his cheek and running off. She wasn't in another scene that day anyway.

Allison raced home. The moment she was in the house, she used her cell phone to look up Miss Jankowski. She found a local number matching the name almost immediately. She called and waited for someone to pick up.

A very feminine, "Hello?" was what she received.

"Is this Janine Jankowski?" she asked.

"This is she," responded the woman. "Who's calling?"

"Allison Jennings," Allison stated firmly, even though she knew that she was going to get herself into so much trouble.

The reaction was instant. "What?!" the woman yelled. "Slater told me that I was an anonymous source!"

Allison managed to laugh lightly. "I have my connections," she said. "Don't worry, Miss Jankowski. You will stay utterly anonymous, if you give me some answers."

"Okay."

Allison steadied herself and then asked the question that was weighing heaviest on her mind. "What can you tell me about Ethan and his police record?" she asked, her voice hushed. She felt so guilty, but she had a right to know. He had slept with her and she was falling in love with him again. It was only natural.

"Ethan was arrested two years ago," the girl responded matter-of-factly. "There was a huge drug bust at this party. Stuff was being given to minors too. He's a bad person, sweetie, and I only talked to Slater in hopes that the message would get out to you. If he's staying with you, he's going to use your fame. You're a very talented actress, you know?"

"I'm aware," Allison scoffed. Usually, she did not have that type of attitude, but she was feeling rather threatened. "Is he really an addict?"

"I can only assume."

"He's homeless..."

"That's what happens to those kinds," the girl sighed. "He's using you, honey."

"He's using me?" she asked.

"Undoubtedly. That's what he does to girls. Trust me, I'm a first-hand source. If he can get some recognition, some money, then he'll dump you at the curb. I knew him closely. Don't trust him."

"I don't trust him!" Allison suddenly yelled.

"Is that all you need?" the girl asked.

"Mhm."

"Well, it was nice talking to you, Miss Jennings. I'm a big fan. Goodbye."

Allison hung up, feeling sick to her stomach. It seemed the evidence was overwhelming in favor of Ethan being a drug addicted criminal who was using her. She just did not want to believe it. She looked up...

...and right into Ethan's eyes.

"So, you don't trust me?" Ethan asked. He held up something. In his hand was a copy of the tabloid. "You don't trust me because of this, I assume?"

Allison took a step towards Ethan. His green eyes were full of what could only be described as hurt. She remembered the rush of pleasure that had overcome her as they made love the night before.

"Ethan, what am I supposed to think?" she asked. "You're homeless and only come to me after ten years because you need a place to stay. Then, this leaks and I talked to Slater's source. Slater's sources are...statistically right."

Ethan's eyes were hard, cold. Allison did not know what to believe.

"Ethan, I've always had to protect myself. I started this career young, female and alone. People take advantage..."

"What's the name of Slater's source?" he asked.

"Janine Jankowski," she whispered.

Ethan's cold eyes morphed then. There was something almost humorous in them.

He laughed. "Tell me, sweetie, was I your only ex-boyfriend?"

Not understanding his question, Allison shook her head. "Of course not," she frowned. Ethan was far from the last boy or man that she had dated in her lifetime. She had probably four ex-boyfriends in her life, actually.

Ethan took a step forward and put his hand on her shoulder. She flinched slightly, but could not bring herself to pull away. "Do you think that they'd say good things about you, if I called them right now?" he asked.

Allison shook her head. No, Ethan had not been the last boyfriend that she had been selfish and slightly oblivious with. Her second boyfriend, Paul, would probably call her by names that would make even the boldest man blush. Relationships always had a chance to end badly and when they did, people did not think nicely of the ex who broke their heart.

"Janine is my ex-girlfriend," Ethan told her. "She's my most recent ex, actually. We broke up very badly. There was a party, about just over two years ago. It was busted for drugs. I was arrested, but I wasn't using that night. Unfortunately, it was at my apartment. The stuff was on my property, but I didn't do anything about it. Got myself a record that night. Janine's brother, Johanne, had stuff on his person. He got it worse than anyone. Janine has always been pissed off because I didn't help him hide in my apartment. I think you could say that she hates my guts."

Ethan's words were heavy but they shook slightly. He was angry and depressed.

"People never tell you how much even a misdemeanor drug charge can screw you up in the employment world," he said meaningfully. "I then fell onto some hard times. I lost my job, lost my apartment. Since then I have managed to develop some better friendships. And I'll have a new apartment by the end of the month. Goodbye Allison. I'm leaving, so you don't have to put up with me. Sorry to have caused you so much unnecessary trouble. "

Ethan pivoted on his foot and walked the other way.

Realizing what she had done, Allison rushed after him and put a hand on his shoulder. Ethan stopped, turned around, forcing her to let go of his shoulder.

"Sorry, Allison, I don't need to deal with this," he said. "Thank you for letting me stay for a couple of nights. I really appreciate it. I was able to clean up and look good at the meetings I attended and that meant a lot. I am, however, done with lies."

Allison did the only thing she could think of. She leaned over and pressed her lips to Ethan's. Tears filled her eyes because she felt really stupid. All her life, she had been taught that she had to stay on guard. Her mentor in the business had told her that explicitly. She was young, relatively pretty and talented. She was female and had a look about her that was naive. People would take advantage.

Allison knew in her heart, however, one man who would never take advantage.

"Do you remember what I always used to say to you?" she asked as she pulled away from the kiss. "Ethan, do you remember?"

"Of course I do," he said, hands sliding down to her waist and holding her. He still looked a little frightened. The anxiety in his eyes reminded her of her own constant vigilance against a world out to get her.

Nineteen year old Allison Jennings was many things. She was rash, impulsive and could get lost in herself for days. She was selfish, at times, but also had a big heart. She was, above all things, a hopeless romantic. She believed in love and giving herself completely to whatever she did. Whether it was show business, her family or the boy she loved, Allison gave all of her heart.

It was the first time that she had made love with her boyfriend, Ethan, and the first time she had ever made real love. Allison lay in his arms, holding him tightly to her. "Ethan," she had muttered against the curve of his neck. "I love you with all of my heart."

"Can I say it again?" she asked, feeling guilty for what she had begun to assume, but determined to do so.

Ethan nodded.

"I love you with all of my heart Ethan," she whispered. "Can we try to love like that again?"

He held her tight and kissed her again. Allison knew she really did love him, and that she could also trust him with all of her heart.

Book 2

Patsy yawned and stretched, as she looked at the clock hanging on the wall of the old fifties-style diner. She had met her friends for lunch and had really been enjoying herself, but now the twenty four year old student was absolutely exhausted.

She supposed that was because she was a busy woman. She worked long hours, was in school to become an occupational therapist and was also very socially active, or at least as much as she could manage. It was a busy life she led, but a good one. She could definitely say that she was happy.

"I hate to run," she told her two friends, Matt and Sarah, whom she had been visiting. "I have had such a long day. I'll catch up with you guys really soon."

Sarah smiled at her. "See you soon Pat," she nodded with a grin. "It's nice to finally steal you from your busy schedule."

"Well, I appreciate being stolen," Patsy assured them.

She hugged both Matt and Sarah and then took the short walk back to the flat she shared with two other girls. The place was small for three young women, but Patsy was simultaneously blessed and cursed by the fact that her two roommates were just as busy as she was. She didn't see them that often, but when she did they all got along very well. It was a perfect living situation.

The building she lived in was also really pleasant. It was a small complex with twenty or so units. Several of her neighbours were students from the same school Patsy attended, but there were also others. It was in a quiet neighbourhood and there was no major trouble. That had been one thing that had scared her when she moved out from her parents and went to live on her own, but there was no such trouble.

As she headed in, Patsy noticed a man. He was heading into the unit across from hers with a large box. He set it down and then started to head towards the sidewalk, where other boxes were stacked. It was obvious that he was moving in. Patsy remembered that the couple who'd lived in that unit, 1F, had left a month earlier. He must be the new resident. She noticed how pronounced his limp was, and walked over to where he was dragging in the boxes.

"Need a hand?" Patsy asked quickly. She was exhausted, but the poor guy obviously wasn't in tip-top physical condition and if he was moving in that was no easy task at all.

The man looked up at her. His reply was quick and snippy.

"No, I don't need your help," he barked in a deep, gruff voice. "I am just fine, thank you very much." He just glared at her and seemed to stare her down.

The rude response fell on Patsy in a delayed manner, because she was caught up looking into his eyes. The stranger had the most wonderful coloured soft amber eyes. They were layered in brown and gold hues and... well, just beautiful eyes. The man was young too. He didn't look much older than her, despite a face that had clearly been aged with pain.

"Sorry," she mumbled awkwardly.

"Yeah, understandable, I guess," he huffed before walking off. Patsy was definitely curious about that man.

"Well, welcome to the neighbourhood," she called after him, more than a little irritated by his rudeness. She knew that some people were anything but personable, but the fact that he was so rude to someone trying to help him out definitely rubbed her the wrong way. What was his deal? It almost seemed scary. She shivered for a few seconds.

When she entered her own apartment, Patsy found it was empty. Her two roommates Katie and Cassie were out. She was happy about that, whereas the silence usually disturbed her. She needed a few moments just to relax, so walked into the bedroom that she'd claimed as her own and took off her jacket.

As she slowly stripped off her clothing, Patsy checked herself out in the mirror. She was definitely not bad looking, despite the tired look in her eyes. Her hair was an auburn-red. Sometimes it hung a little too limply for her taste, but today she'd curled it up nicely. She wasn't skinny, or fat. Her body type was somewhere in the middle of things. She had curves in her hips and breasts. The only part that she didn't much like about herself was that she was rather pale, with freckles dotting her skin. She stripped off her shirt, revealing those very spots. Then taking off the rest of her clothes, she dumped them in the hamper in the bathroom and turned on the bath taps.

She listened to the steady stream of water and once there was at least an inch in the tub, she slipped on in. Letting out a sigh, Patsy leaned back, getting her hair wet. It looked blood red when she leaned into the water. She closed her eyes and relaxed, muscles turning into mush in the water. Again a soft sigh of obvious pleasure.

"Mm, very good," she exhaled out loudly as she let the water finish filling.

She shut off the water when it was done. Lying in the bath, taking deep steamy breaths, she just relaxed. Her mind wandered back to the new neighbour.

He was so attractive and wow, those eyes. Inwardly, Patsy rolled her eyes at herself. It had been way too long since she'd had a good date.. that was what it was. Her lack of time and energy had led to her avoiding men for the most part and she was probably thinking about the handsome stranger because she'd been on a massive dry spell. She hadn't even dated a man in the past two years!

After a long, luxurious bath Patsy finally got out and dried herself. She put on her pyjamas and a bathrobe and then sat at the end of her bed, drying her hair. No sooner did she start doing that, when her roommate Cassie showed up.

The girl was a short, spunky blonde with a pixie cut. "Heya Patsy!" she declared as she entered. Patsy wondered how the other girl knew she was home. Then again, she was the one of the three girls who was always home. She didn't go out as much as the other two girls.

Patsy walked out, not minding that her friend saw her in her pyjamas.

"Hey," she said with a grin. "How are you?"

"I'm not bad," Cassie replied, putting her things up and looking at Patsy with a yawn.

They talked for awhile about simple, mundane things and then Patsy brought up the subject of the new man across the way.

"Have you heard anything about the new guy?" she asked. "The guy in 1F? I saw him earlier today and I was just wondering about him..."

She tried not to sound like some idiot girl who hadn't seen a handsome man in years.

Cassie smiled at her words. "Oh the handsome one?" she asked. "Katie says that he's ex-army. He was wounded in battle and is recovering."

"Oh, maybe that explains things," Patsy murmured.

"Like?"

"Oh," she explained with a slight laugh. "He was rude to me when I asked him if he needed any help and he was limping pretty badly when I saw him."

"He's really handsome," Cassie laughed. "Maybe you should go get some of that."

Patsy threw a pillow at her.

Patsy did not really think about the mysterious former soldier living across the hallway after that. She was so busy with school, work and her attempts at maintaining a social life, that he went right out of her mind. He was a handsome face, but there was little more to him than that. He wasn't even important enough to fall on her radar.

About a week after her first sighting of him, however, Patsy was heading home past his apartment, when she heard a loud crash. It sounded as if something like glass had fallen and had just shattered. She heard a faintly gasped curse in a deep, masculine voice. She paused to listen. That was when she realized that the door was slightly ajar.

"Are you okay in there?" she called, leaning up close to the slightly opened door.

There was no reply, so she peered inside.

Patsy knew that it was an idiotic thing to do which went against every lesson on both safety and politeness that a young girl had ever learnt in her life. She just wanted to make sure that the man was all right. He was a wounded army veteran. For all she knew, he could have fallen or something and she could be saving his life. It only made sense for her to try and intervene - didn't it?

It wasn't exactly a life-or-death situation that Patsy walked in on. The man was standing in his kitchen, where a large sized glass vase had broken into thousands of tiny little shards of glass. The fake flowers that had been inside of the vase were also scattered through the glass on the floor.

"I'm sorry," she exclaimed as she backed off, realizing that her intrusiveness was probably at least a little bit rude. "I just heard a crash and was worried someone got hurt."

"Nobody but my pride," the man growled in a dazed voice, as he looked up at her. His deep amber eyes were emphasized by his furrowed brow as he started to sweep up the glass with a broom. Patsy noticed a dust pan sitting near his washing machine and walked over and grabbed it.

"Thanks for caring, I guess," he muttered to her.

Patsy quickly held the dustpan so the ex-soldier could sweep the glass shards into it.

"These flowers are pretty," she smiled, as she carefully picked them out from the glass, trying not to cut herself. "You should put them in a bit sturdier vase if you have one."

"The vase was sturdy," the man emphasised, his voice still gruff and full of some kind of incomprehensible hurt. "My hands weren't."

"Oh," Patsy acknowledged, his words making her feel awkward at best. She quickly started to clean up the shards with him, working without meeting his eyes completely. She was a little embarrassed by her own intrusive behaviour and wished she'd minded her own business.

"You're quite helpful, miss," he quipped in a way that she was sure was making fun of her and that made her blush.

She rolled her eyes. "It's in my way."

"You live across the hall," he commented, as if it was just the most random fact. "What's your name?"

She stood up when the shards of glass were all swept up. "Patsy," she told him.

"Old fashioned, country girl?" he queried with a slight almost-laugh.

"Oh no, and what's your name if I dare ask?" she looked at him, her eyes flaring with the intense banter between the two.

"Aiden."

"Modern, sounds like it belongs on a hipster teenage boy," she responded, smiling.

"Touche," he almost laughed. It sounded like he wanted to laugh but was prevented by a roadblock of some kind.

"Well," she mumbled awkwardly. There was an obvious chemistry between the two of them, but she felt intrusive, like she needed to get out of his house. "Since you now know that I have a tendency to be very helpful, I'm just across the hall if you need any help."

She decided quickly that this was the easiest way to dismiss herself and get out of there quickly.

"I don't need help," he said firmly, like that declaration meant so much. "I am quite capable on my own."

"All right then," she murmured. "See ya."

Patsy took off quickly after that, trying to diffuse the awkwardness. Still, now something had been piqued inside of her and she wanted to know more about this Aiden. There was something about him that was incredibly strong, but incredibly needy at the same time. He had this fighting spirit and she found that now he was more than a pretty face. He was more than the random crush she had on a handsome man. Now she wanted to know who he was.

A few nights later, Patsy tried to get her mind off of her new neighbour by attending a friend's house party. Her roommates were now convinced that she desperately needed to meet a man and who knew? Maybe she would. She was, however, the slightest bit uncomfortable when she entered the large house. The music was loud and distracting and although she saw familiar faces, she was never too great with crowds.

After a moment, however, she found Katie, who had left for the party before her. "Glad you coul come, sweetie," Katie said with a grin, as she gestured over to the table where drinks were being served. "Grab a drink, Pat; let's have some fun."

Patsy slowly loosened up. She had a couple of drinks and danced with Katie and some of her other friends. She felt like a total goof dancing, but a couple of drinks were enough to loosen her up enough to at least curb the hot blush on her face whenever she danced around with the others. She was giggling as she danced.

Then, Patsy looked over Katie's shoulder and noticed something that absolutely stunned her. He was there. Yes, Aiden, the man who lived across the hall from her was at the party. He was standing alone near a corner of the room, looking so uncomfortable and out of place. He ran a hand through his hair and his soft amber eyes were flickering from side to side. He looked like a trapped animal, who wanted nothing more than to get out of there and escape..

"What is it Patsy?" Katie asked.

"Look," she said, gesturing with just her head. "That's our neighbour from across the hall. What's he doing here?"

Eventually, she found out through a friend-of-a-friend, that the girl throwing the party was friends with Aiden's older sister. He seemed so uncomfortable that she wanted to go over and talk to him, but nerves told her otherwise. She did not go up to him immediately.

Then he caught her eye and gave her an odd sort of half-smile, but he did not approach. Patsy was pretty sure they weren't even going to talk until she and Katie split up for a while and she was standing alone.

Patsy was standing near the drinks when she was suddenly approached by two men. They were tall, beefy sort of guys. They seemed to be around her age, or maybe even younger. Both had too much to drink and seemed completely wasted.

"You're hot, Baby" one of them stated, like it was pure fact. "You're hot. I'm hot. I think we should make something of that."

"Unless she wants a real man like me," said the other, putting his big hand on her shoulder. She immediately jerked away. "Chicks don't want fake studs like you, bro."

"Oh she wants it, man. I can tell," the guy objected.

"Who do you want?" the second man said. He touched her and she backed away.

"I want the two of you to get lost," Patsy said, looking around. It wasn't like these idiots were going to pull anything in a crowded room, but still their antics left her feeling somewhat intimidated. Who the hell did they think they were? It was such a typical male attitude, thinking that you were entitled to any poor female who happened to be alone. "Get out of here!"

"Look at the way you're dressed," he scoffed. "You obviously came hoping to get some tonight and guess what? It's your lucky day."

Patsy shook her head. "Even if I wanted to get some..." she began, using his own crude terminology and taking a step forward. Her tone was commanding and it obviously wasn't something that he expected. "Even if I wanted to get some, it would be from a man, not a little boy. Do you understand what I'm saying?"

There was a step behind her and she turned to see Aiden standing next to her. He grabbed the first guy, who could only be described as a total 'bro' in Patsy's mind, and held him by the collar of his white t-shirt. "I think the lady's made her point, don't you?" he growled.

"Psycho bitch," scoffed the second and rushed off.

The moment Aiden let the first free, he followed suit.

Patsy swivelled on a foot and looked at Aiden. "I was handling them myself," she said, unable to keep the small smile off of her face. "Thank you, though. That was very sweet."

Aiden was actually smiling at that moment. It was just a faint smile and there seemed to be that road block up again inside of him, but he was clearly pleased.

"I knew you were handling them just fine," he told her with a slight laugh. "I just have all this aggression inside me, and I found a perfect opportunity to use it. Nobody would fault me for that, thanks to my being a combat veteran and all. It seemed as good an opportunity as any."

Patsy couldn't keep the small smile off of her own face. He was definitely a little calmer, a little less intense and she appreciated it a lot.

"Well, I do thank you," she said with a dramatic sweep of her arm. He laughed, just a little, and it was very worth it. "So, what brought you to this lovely affair anyway?"

Aiden shrugged his shoulders lightly. "My sister's friends with the girl who threw the party," he explained. "They both said that I need to come and have some fun or something like that. I didn't really want to, but they insisted, so I eventually gave up and agreed with them."

"Having fun?" she asked with a slightly hopeful expression.

"Well, I wasn't having much fun," he said honestly, "until right now."

She laughed at that.

He walked over to the table to get a drink and she followed. She watched as he took the bottle in hand and looked at her. He had a soft expression on his face that wasn't quite a smile, but she felt that with a little prodding it could get there. She had a feeling that the wounded army veteran had not smiled very often in recent months. She felt that it was her duty to bring about a smile or two, and she determined to try.

"You look very pretty," he said, his words immediate and surprising.

"Oh, thank you," Patsy replied, finding the blush on her face to be just the slightest bit stupid. It was just a nice, genuine compliment. "You look very nice yourself."

"I tried," the man said with a bitter sounding laugh. "I really haven't been much at putting myself together in these last couple of months."

"Well you've done well," Patsy assured him.

For a moment, the pair looked at each other and didn't say much more. Patsy looked down at her own mostly finished drink and took a little sip, trying to stall for time. Finally, the man broke the silence that had formed between the two of them.

"So what about you?" he asked. "What do you do?"

Patsy always felt a little bit weird talking about herself, but she tried her very best. She looked him directly into those beautiful eyes that reminded her of soft honey. "I'm in school still, for occupational therapy," she said. "I also work part time at a doctor's office as a receptionist. I'm pretty busy most of the time, but I try and have fun." She rolled her eyes and gestured around the party. "See, fun?"

"Oh so much fun," he said, and his expression made her smile. "You go to school around here?"

"Yes," she replied.

"I've been thinking of going to school actually," the man said and briefly, Patsy wondered if he'd be so open and honest if not for the couple of drinks he seemed to have had. "I was injured in Afghanistan last year. Shot here." He gestured to his right hip. "I know my limp is absolutely charming, but it cut my military career a bit short."

"There are always other options," she said cheerfully as she walked across the room to sit down on one of the sofas. He followed her, sitting close by. "I can't even imagine the things that you've been through, but you'll definitely find the path for you. I believe in you."

The man chuckled as he adjusted in his seat. "I suppose you're right," he said. "You're a very cheery person, aren't you?"

"Sometimes," she said, shaking her head. "Sorry."

"No, don't apologize," he said with a nod. "I'm definitely an old grouch, ever since I came home. You don't wanna mess with a man who's twenty-six going on fifty-five, dear."

"I'm sure you're not going on fifty-five," she said, shaking her head at him and playfully rolling her eyes. She nudged him on the shoulder. "Also, who says that I'm messing with you?"

"You keep looking at my lips," he pointed out bluntly.

Patsy blushed a fierce red and looked up at his eyes. She realized then that yes, she had been staring at his lips. The man next to her had supple, soft looking lips and yes, maybe for a minute she was thinking about what it would feel like to kiss them. That still did not mean that she was thinking about kissing him. That did not mean that she intended to try kissing him. She was not that kind.

"I'm not-"

He cut her off by pressing his lips to hers. He kissed her gently, reaching over and cupping her cheek with a big, warm hand. He kissed her lips softly, delicately, but he let it linger all the same. When he pulled back, he was staring into her eyes with a stern expression, but there was a hint of mischief in the way that his eyes twinkled. "Is that what you wanted me to do?" he asked her.

Patsy's first instinct was to say that of course, it was not. She then realized that lying probably wasn't going to work with this man, so she nodded. "Yeah, it was," she told him bluntly, "so can we do it again?"

When he kissed her again it was with a little more intensity. He pressed against her and she practically had to lean back against the sofa. They made out heatedly, all lips and tongues and she could feel the breath being stolen from her. Her entire body was on fire, an electric sort of energy.

"You know, we're not far from the apartment," she suggested. "Do you mind a walk?"

"Not at all," he said with a nod. "My Physical Therapist is always telling me that I need to start taking short walks. Do you mind that I'm a little slow?"

"Not at all."

The walk home was a very pleasant one. Patsy even got Aiden to hold her hand as they walked carefully back towards their apartment. She was eager to leave the loud, annoying party behind. Her heart was thrumming loudly enough in her head, after all. She was not sure what was going to happen between the two of them, but honestly, that part intrigued her. She had never really had an adventurous time with a man and maybe the not knowing was the exciting part.

Without words or an agreement of any kind between them, they went to 1F, rather than to Patsy's apartment. That was best, considering that she had roommates. While it was true that her roommates probably would not return from the party for several hours, it was still safest. Aiden fumbled with his key and after that they quickly walked into his apartment.

Aiden's apartment, now that she was looking at it a bit more closely, was furnished sparingly, but it was still cute in it's own way. In the days since she'd last been in it, the ex-soldier had put up photographs of his family and of other men in army uniform. They headed to Aiden's bedroom, where a very nice four-poster bed sat in the middle of a room that also had a television and a bookshelf.

Her examination of the room concluded when Aiden walked her back towards the bed. She sat down on its edge and he carefully moved between her slightly spread legs, leaning over and kissing her hungrily. She kissed him back, feeling a warmth flood her entire being. He slid his hands over her shoulders and rested them at the small of her back as they continued to kiss. "You are such a beautiful woman," he groaned, as if he had never seen a woman he found attractive before. She had to admit that the reverent way he spoke about her was enough to drive her a little crazy.

His lips left hers for a moment, but they quickly found a new spot at the corner of her mouth. He trailed kisses down her chin, to her jaw and to the corner of her neck. He was detailed, meticulous with getting every inch of flesh in his grasp. She let out a moan of pleasure and fell back against the bed. She reached out and touched his chest, fingers slipping underneath the fabric of his t-shirt. Under his shirt, she ran her fingers over raw, defined muscle. He was so strong.

Aiden encouraged her to take off his shirt, so she did, slipping it up over his head. He took it off the rest of the way and cast it aside. Her eyes took in every inch of defined muscle that she'd felt. The way he'd dressed had hidden the muscular body underneath.

"Wow," she whispered, unable to hide the childish way that she was impressed by the man she was looking at.

"Glad you approve," he murmured.

He left his space between her legs and moved to the top of the bed, near the headboard. She scrambled to follow him there. They kissed again, both on their knees on the bed. He looked at her questioningly as he started to strip off her shirt. She nodded and he took it off. She felt exposed in just a lacy black bra, but at the same time the vulnerability was thrilling. She'd only let one other man into this position and the fact that she was letting another was amazing to her. She cast aside her skirt too, before she could get nervous and back out. She was glad she'd chosen nice undergarments in that moment. She looked good.

He kissed her heatedly as the rest of the clothes came off. When he was stripped down to a pair of red boxer shorts, she could see what effect she was having on him and that was utterly enthralling. She tugged him closer, using a firm hold on his bicep. He kissed her deeply, plundering her mouth with a skilled tongue. She gasped and tilted her head back with a groan.

They hit the bed at once. She was beneath him and giggled as her back hit the fabric. He straddled her hips and leaned over. He was determined and fierce, not at all too gentle and she liked that a lot. He pressed his hips to hers. They were both only clothed in undergarments and the light thrust of his hips made her gasp pathetically.

"Oh god, so good..." she said, trying to encourage him to give her more. He did just what she asked and moved again.

"We need..." she told him, not even finishing her sentence.

He took off her bra with delicate hands that shook just slightly. He managed the task quickly however, and then took to touching her with mouth and finger. Her pleasure was obviously the first thing on his mind. His fingers trailed over her collarbone while his mouth found her right breast, teasing with delicate touches of lip and tongue. His tongue swirled lightly around her nipple while he stroked her collarbone. He moved both his mouth and his hands all along her chest, neck and shoulders. His hand eventually found its way to her stomach and then to the waistband of her panties.

He touched her with delicate hands until she was practically begging for him. "Ungh," she said. "I need…" Her half-hearted begging eventually turned into full on begging. "Please, I need it." Her new lover was happy to oblige. As she touched him, stroking along his chest and abs, he retrieved a condom from somewhere in the bedside drawer. They kissed heatedly, enjoying each languid movement of tongue and lips, until he took down her underwear and slid his fingers over her skin as he took them down her legs, discarding them completely.

"Please," she said again.

When he finally entered her, it was bliss and completion all rolled up into one delicious package. He moved slowly until he bottomed out and then he stilled. She presumed that was for her benefit and leant up, kissing the junction between his neck and shoulder.

"'M good," she assured, wanting him to start moving and not go easy on her at all.

He seemed to pick up on that as he began to move. Each thrust of his hips was firm and deep. She couldn't help the breathy moans that escaped her at that.

"Oh!" she cried out.

He thrust deep and hard. As he did, she moved her hands up and down his sides, over his strong shoulders, where she clutched tightly. She met his thrusts with her hips, moaning out desperately as he seemed to find the perfect angle to have his partner seeing stars. The friction was absolutely brilliant.

He was a pretty quiet lover, but that didn't make him bad at his job; no, not at all. Actually, she appreciated the small, quiet cues that what she did pleased him. She nipped at the skin of his neck and instead of a loud moan to tell her that he enjoyed it, she felt a shudder of pleasure go through his entire body. He made small sounds too, gasps and whimpers of delight. She appreciated the subtleties.

When he eventually peaked, it was also subtle. His eyes shut tightly and he let out a small gasp that sounded like a release of pent up tension.

"Ah…." he gasped out and then stopped thrusting steadily into her. He stilled and then pulled back while he was still shaking a little. She could detect the faintest tremor in his body and she loved that. She was almost too busy watching him when he pulled out and touched her. His fingers worked magic.

After a moment she closed her eyes and the world exploded for just a split second. She tensed and everything was hot and wet and perfect. She knew she screamed, but she wasn't at all embarrassed by the action. It was only natural.

"Oh ... oh wow..." she whispered as she came down, trying her best to just catch her breath. "Oh wow."

It was amazing, and shortly after both parties drifted off into an amazing sleep. Patsy fell asleep in his arms in a sweaty, sticky puddle of bliss. She did not think anything could get better. She just didn't imagine, however, that when she woke up the next morning, that she would be alone.

When she woke up, Patsy was alone in a strange man's apartment. The bed was empty except for her body. Aiden was nowhere to be seen. She sat up and stretched, only to find a note lying on the bedside table. It was written in shaky scratchy writing that was almost difficult to read.

It read: *Sorry about last night. I had to go out. Feel free to lock up when you leave.*

"Sorry about last night?" she whispered.

Patsy could not describe how very burnt she felt by those words. He was sorry? He had given her a fantastic, wonderful night and all he could really tell her was that he was sorry? It hadn't exactly been a one-sided affair. Maybe he wasn't in love with her and that was okay, but that didn't give him the right to run off with just an apologetic note saying that he was sorry. She was okay with casual sex, but she expected a little bit of honesty in the whole affair.

"Way to make a girl feel cheap..." she muttered.

Quickly, Patsy dressed and left his apartment. She just wanted to get out of that situation as fast as she could. Unfortunately, she was not alone when she opened her door and walked inside. Cassie was in the kitchen, drinking from what smelled like a rather strong cup of coffee.

"I knew it!" Cassie squealed with juvenile delight when she walked into the room.

"Knew what?" Patsy grumbled.

Cassie giggled as though she was all of twelve years old. "You and the handsome soldier," she said with a drawl. "I saw you two leaving last night and I knew you went back to his place. How good was he?"

"Shut up."

Cassie chuckled softly, shaking her head over her mug. "Okay, okay," she said, putting up a hand. "Don't have to kiss and tell Pat. I would've done the same."

Patsy rolled her eyes. She couldn't help her bad mood. She got up and walked to her bedroom. It was disappointing that she'd had such a wonderful night with a man and he'd just dismissed her so rudely. She ran a hand through her hair and then changed her clothes. She wanted nothing more than to get out of her mussed up party clothes and into something casual. Once she had switched to a simple jeans and t-shirt combination, she decided that she couldn't hang around the apartment. She decided to go for a walk.

Ignoring Cassie, she left the apartment only a few minutes after she'd arrived. She walked up the street to a local park. It was small, but had a path that wound around an artificial lake. It was a good place for taking a stroll and clearing one's mind of things one would rather not be thinking about. Patsy definitely had a lot that she did not want to be thinking about in that moment.

For a little while, her idea was a good one. For a little while, she was able to walk around the little lake and forget. It was when she turned up a tiny path that went in towards the lake that she saw him standing there. He was wearing a white button down shirt and jeans and was leaning on a park bench. He was staring out into the lake as if the clear water could give him some kind of answer. He did not see her. She was standing behind him. Patsy was very free, in that moment, to just walk past him and forget she'd seen him there.

She really wasn't that kind of woman, however. She was strong, independent and she was angry.

"Do you leave all your lovers with a dismissive note?" she asked, approaching him swiftly. "That's rude."

He swivelled around on his good leg and stared at her with wide eyes. "Did you follow me?" he demanded.

"No," she said coldly. "I just figured that I needed to take a walk after your apology of a letter."

Aiden stared at her without making a sound. He lifted a hand and opened his mouth but said nothing. Patsy could sense a hesitance to his gesture.

Finally he spoke. "Don't get worked up over it," he said, shaking his head. "It was a one night thing. It was pretty stupid on both our parts."

Patsy winced at his words, but tried to act as though they had no effect. "Pretty stupid, sure," she said, "but pretty cowardly to run out on me."

He took a limping step towards her and groaned. "Don't be like that," he said. "I shouldn't have had sex with anyone. I'm not exactly whole. Damaged men aren't supposed to get involved." He took a few more limping steps then slammed his fist on the bench, crossed over and sat down. She could tell that he was in a bit of physical pain, in addition to what must have been some pretty heavy emotional turmoil.

Patsy thought sincerely about walking out again, but instead crossed in front of the bench and sat beside him. "Damaged men?" she asked.

Aiden laughed at that. His laugh was bitter and cold, but it too seemed to be forced.

"Sweetie, you don't have to stretch your imagination too hard to figure that one out," he said. His tone would have been condescending and awful to hear from anyone else, but she could tell that he was hurting deeply.

"Ex-soldier here. I'm a bit more damaged than a screwed up leg. My head's not on straight. You're lucky I didn't wake you up last night with a nightmare, or an episode or whatever."

"That makes you hurt, not damaged..." she said, turning to face him.

The man opened his mouth to yell at her. Patsy even braced herself for the verbal blow, but instead he shook his head.

"I wanted to get back to a normal life," he admitted to her. "Going to parties, going back to school, having sex with beautiful, sweet, regular girls, but I'm not normal."

"And I'm not regular," she said.

Her words caused a strange look to flicker over the man's features. He looked at her a few times, glancing away in between small gazes.

"No, you're not," he said softly, reaching over towards her. She responded by boldly taking his hand in hers. She didn't know what she felt about him yet, but that spark was still there. It was stronger than it had ever been and it was always worth exploring when there was a true spark.

"Can I kiss you?" Patsy asked. It was a delicate question, because she knew that she wanted to try this, to try to take them further, but she knew he was so afraid, so hesitant to bridge that gap. Maybe he would decide that it wasn't worth it and that he was going to leave the night they shared as a one night stand, a hook-up. That would be okay too, but by gosh, she wanted him to let her in emotionally. "Please, Aiden?"

The man nodded. It was barely a nod.

She leaned over and pressed her lips to his. The kiss was gentle and chaste, considering the fact that they'd already explosively made love. It was Patsy's quiet way of telling him that she did not see him as damaged, just hurt and in need. It was her way of telling him that she wasn't certain of what they were or would be, but that there was a spark and there were feelings. It was her way of saying that she was giving it her all and she'd like his all too.

Aiden felt the warmth in her kiss. He felt his damaged heart was not beyond repair. This girl was different. If anyone could, Aiden knew that she was the one to rekindle that spark.

Through his kiss, he told her that he didn't know what his all was, but he would try and give it to her. Then they kissed again. And this time Aiden knew. He could fall in love, and he felt his heart leap for the first time. Yes, he was falling in love with the girl who had saved him.

Patsy felt the change too, looked into his eyes, smiled and kissed him strongly and firmly. She felt so relaxed and overjoyed. She was falling in love too.

Book 3

What Older Women Say

"Older women are best, because they always think they may be doing it for the last time."

- Ian Fleming

A Cougar In The Wild

This is a factual account written by a mature woman for mature women. I can just imagine that there are a lot of women who are in my age group. I am a sexagenarian.

These women may be single, divorced or widowed and think that after a certain age, sex is not even on the table as by that time the sex appeal that they used to have would have been long gone. Let me tell you that that is a crock of baloney. I am aware of this as I thought the same thing for two years after I turned sixty. Everything changed when I turned sixty-two.

The man who I was married to since we graduated from college died of medical complications at the age of fifty six. I was so upset with everyone for about a year.

My anger then morphed into self-pity and nothing anyone could say would make me feel good about myself or my situation. Thankfully when it was three years after my husband's death that I started to recover and rediscover the world and my friends. I accepted who I was and where I was. That is how my fantastic story begins, with healing.

The process involved me starting to exercise again. I managed to shed the excess weight I had gained. I also got my hair styled and even put in some risqué highlights. I did some more tweaks to my body and went to a doctor who removed my ugly varicose veins. I also had a breast lift and a tummy tuck as no amount of exercise would fix those problems.

I was going to be sixty two and I wanted to be fully secure with myself. Come on now, I was not ready for a beauty competition by any means, I could lose some more weight and at that age wrinkles take over. I was, however at a more comfortable place with myself.

Soon after this revamping of self, things started to happen. I was out to have lunch with friends and I was waiting for them as I had gotten there early. It was a nice day so I opted for outside seating.

I soon realized that a young man was making a concerted effort to look up my skirt. I smiled to myself thinking that it was a plus that any man; old or young would be interested in an old bird like me. I suddenly realized that he was only trying to get a glimpse of my underwear or my vagina. That was the moment that I became a bit of an exhibitionist.

I had a wonderful lunch with the girls. When I was driving home I kept on thinking about the young man. I wondered what he would have really done to me if he had the opportunity to see my vagina. Would it be a good enough rush for him to go and masturbate. I could think of nothing else but him in his room masturbating with that picture in his head until he came. It was such an intense thought that I was getting wet myself. I could feel that my panties were soaked.

When I got home I would have to masturbate. I drove in to the garage, ensured it was closed and I got out and masturbated right there in the garage. Since my husband's death I had set up a nice little hobby corner for myself so I had ample room to work. I didn't take long to come. Who would have thought that this would ever happen? I was pretty straight laced and never ever thought I was that sexual woman. I had never initiated sex in my marriage. I did not hate sex but there is so much and no more you can do or so I thought. I may be over sixty but I had a lot to learn.

I still thought about the young man for the next few days. I had a very vivid imagination and in my mind, I saw him trying to see my vagina. Since I saw him that day and after masturbating in the garage, I shaved when I was getting ready for bed. I was still fantasizing and I saw him and how he was looking at me. I was motivated by his look to open my legs slowly and reveal myself to him. He started to rub his dick.

No matter what I did, the vision was stuck in my head. I fantasized so much that I was now planning how I could make that a reality. The first part of the plan involved the restaurant where I had first seen the young man. I was going to go back there.

I had been shopping recently so I had options. I was going to just go and I was not going to wear any panties at all. If not him, some other young man would love that view. Of course it was a plan that I was not brave enough to carry out but it was a great fantasy for a day or so.

I ended up going back to the restaurant. I had just come from the hairdresser so my hair was beautiful, the grays were covered and my highlights spruced up. I had on a nice sleeveless mini dress. I wore no panties and no bra. The breast lift was sufficient to keep my breasts up. The lunch rush was already on. I was so excited; this was the most adventurous thing that I have ever done. I put in my order and had an iced tea while I waited. Soon enough, a nice looking young man came in and sat across from me at the next table. He looked over and I crossed my legs.

He kept looking. He looked at my toned legs right up to my freshly done hair and back down. I waited until his gaze went back down and then I seductively uncrossed my legs. He had a full view of my shaved vagina. I saw him look around as if guilty of something. I was making an impression here. He kept on looking as if he could not believe his good luck.

This was a turn on for me. I was now super excited. I was getting wet. This was nasty business and I was enjoying it immensely. Is he to go home and relieve my sexual tension? I asked the waiter to pack my order to go.

I rushed home, thankfully I lived close by and I went into my room and got undressed quickly. I started to fantasize about that young man and I pulled off two orgasms just thinking what he was doing after seeing my vagina.

It became my new rush. It was starting to consume me. I was going through all my clothes and trying to find the sexiest outfits that would flatter my body without me seeming to be a whore or an old biddy trying to recapture her youth. I needed skirts or dresses that would facilitate me flashing these young men. I even went shopping to get clothes that would facilitate that. In my mind I was providing them with a unique experience. Just seeing the look on their faces was enough for me. It was not a look of disgust; it was a look of lust. Those who have never experienced something like this would find it hard to understand what I am saying. To date it is the most sexually adventurous thing I have done outside my home.

I was out shopping yet again and got hungry so I decided to grab a bite to eat at the food court. After I was relaxing and checking my phone when I noticed that a young man, a teenager really was seated close to me. He could not have been more than seventeen and he was having a burger.

I scanned the area to see if anyone else was looking in my direction. I discreetly let my bag fall and as I bent to pick it up I opened my legs so he could see. I had also made it a habit to wear sunglasses to hide my own expression and to be able to look at the person without them realizing. His face changed and I knew he had gotten an eyeful.

I had perfected my technique. I kept on entertaining him. He had finished his burger but he was still sitting there looking right at my vagina with no fear. I could see that his penis was fighting to get free from his pants. I had a great plan in my head. I checked to make sure the area was clear and then I opened my legs again and ran my hand slowly up my thigh. I saw him grab his penis. I had done well as I was sure he had had an orgasm. I went off to finish my shopping.

I was on a high as I headed home. As I got to my room I dropped the packages and masturbated. I was so wet as I thought to myself that I still had enough appeal to make a teenager have an orgasm in his pants. This was my best masturbation session to date. As I came I thought about that teenager coming all over me. I had a big orgasm. I could not move from the bed for a good while.

I reviewed everything that had happened since the lunch with my girls at the restaurant. I was now quite a great exhibitionist but I missed the foreplay and actual sex with another person. I still hungered for something more than that. I had the need to be touched, to be held, to be fucked.

I decided to stay home the next day. I was watching my favorite morning show when I saw a local ad from a carpet cleaning service. They were offering free estimates and they would come in and evaluate to see what had to be done. I thought it was a great idea to clean the carpets and I called to set up the appointment.

On the appointed day I had a nice bath and dressed in a nice shirt and a swing skirt. I put no underwear on. The doorbell rang at exactly 10 am. I answered and outside was a tall, lanky young man who was in his early twenties. Not who I had hoped to see but he will do. He came in and did his inspection of the carpets. He then wanted to update me on what he had outlined. I motioned for him to sit in the chair which I had placed directly in front of the one I would sit in. I was about to put on my show.

I was already excited and my pussy was dripping. I was in uncharted territory here so I let it play out. H sat and started to explain how they would clean the carpets in the most convenient manner. He was also going into costing I suppose but I had stopped listening. I was scared to make my move.

Finally I worked up the guts to just do it. I opened my legs just enough. For him to get a good look and then crossed them. He automatically looked down. He played it cool and went on explaining company procedure. When he was done, I offered him a beverage. He opted to have an iced tea.

It was obvious that I would have to uncross my legs and get up. As I did that I opened my leg wider than before. He did not look away this time. I got his iced tea and when I was heading toward him I noticed that he had an erection which he was not hiding. I sat back down with my legs open acting as if I did not know that he could see my pussy.

He had a hungry look on his face as he took it all in. He was now rubbing his cock and he asked if I would be interested in their services.

I asked if he would be present for the actual cleaning if I decided to go ahead with it. He said no, he was only the front man, he did the estimates and the sales pitch.

The time for talking was over, it way I me to see if he would take the bait. I opened my legs really wide and asked how much time he had now. He indicated that his next appointment was in thirty minutes and if that time would be sufficient. He had leaked pre-cum and it was showing through his light colored pants. I was extremely wet.

"That is enough time," I said.

He came across to me told me to lie back on the sofa and he lifted my skirt and started to lick my pussy. This was heavenly. I was so wet, wetter than I had ever been before. He stuck his tongue deep into my pussy and then licked the labia and went back to my throbbing clit. H even licked my anus. It felt so good. I was losing my mind, I was close to coming.

He sensed that I was close to coming and he pressed down on my clit. He also pushed two fingers in my vagina and worked them as well. He kept on sucking as I came violently, my juices running out of my pussy. He sucked it all up.

That was what I really needed. He then took his pants off. Mind you his dick was not an overwhelming sight but if he knew how to use it, it would suit me just fine. I took his dick in my hands and started to suck it. I had not done this for a long time but it was all coming back to me. I licked the head and worked the base then do took the whole cook in my mouth and moved my head back and forth on it.

With these alternating motions I felt his dick get even harder. He was visibly shaking and his head was thrown back. He had my head pushing me forward onto his dick. He gasped and then came in my mouth. I swallowed every last bit of it before I released his cock. He stroked it a couple times and more juice came out falling onto my stomach. I was lying there with my eyes closed rubbing his cum into my skin when I heard the door close, he was gone.

I kept that up for a while calling various companies for estimates and trying my technique to see who would take the bait. I had success with all of them. My next call was to the air conditioning company. They sent over a tall, dark and extremely handsome technician. He was maybe twenty five or twenty six no more than that.

We went through the usual preliminaries of the estimate and when he sat down to go through the details I did my signature move. I did it quite a few times. He was looking at my pussy without seeming to look. I could tell he was turned on by it. He would not make the first move I knew that so I waited for him to finish his sales speech. I looked at him, lifted up my skirt and said, "I think I could use your services, what do you think?"

He stared at my now wet pussy and said, **"Mam, the sooner we start, the better off you will be."**

I smiled, got up and went toward him. I helped him to his feet and pulled his pants and slid them down. He was in the wrong line of work as he would do well as a porn star. His dick was the hugest I have ever seen. It was beautiful to look at; he was beautiful to look at. I held his dick and it was glorious. I knelt down and started to play with his dick. I used my hand to stroke it and then I started teasing the tip with my tongue and started to suck it. Now this was something I wished I could keep at home. He was almost about o come when he stopped me.

He helped me out of my dress and lay me down on the carpet. He took off the rest of his clothes as well. I opened my legs wide and he positioned himself between them. He used his big dick to rub against my pussy before entering. He grunted in pleasure as his dick slid into my extra wet pussy. He was making me experience thing is never did before. I had heard women speak of the joy of a big dick but this was the first time I was experiencing it for myself. I was on the verge of passing out.

He fucked me like a pro. I started to shake uncontrollably and he increased his pace. I could hardly contain myself a is came. It was so explosive. He kept on thrusting until he came himself. He started to rub my clit again. I was in sensory overdrive at this point. Was I really supposed to be experiencing all this pleasure at my age? His cum was oozing out of my pussy but he did not pull out. He started to thrust again, more slowly this time. I was amazed as I was ready for a long nap after that experience. If felt so good.

He was going to go cum again and he started to thrust faster. When my husband made love to me when he was still able to it never felt like this. I was being fucked for all I was worth and I liked it. He was so big and I could feel him getting even bigger. Was that even possible? I lifted my hips to accommodate him. I stabilized myself and matched him thrust for thrust. We were there fucking on the carpet for a good twenty minutes and then he moaned loudly and started to cum again. He pulled out and moved his dripping dick to my waiting mouth. I could not suck up all the cum, it was a mega load. I just let the rest drip down my cheeks.

He was still shaking. **"If I may say so mam, you know what you are doing."**

I did not bother to move as he got dressed, he let himself out. Surprisingly I was not done. I wanted, needed to cum again so I started rubbing my clit slowly. It was glorious and when I came it was just as explosive as the first one.

I was sore the following morning; my pussy had never experienced a cock that big before so I took that day off to recover. I was still thinking of who would be next. I thrived off the power of seduction that I had. It was about much more than getting sex now. I had morphed into some sort of monster.

It was now fall and it was can nice and cool. I had to dress more modestly but I still could go without panties. I longer to visit the orchard near the home. It would be full of beautiful fall colors. I made the short drive out to the countryside. I went in and enjoyed the beauty of nature. I had not been back here since my husband died. They had a bird sanctuary so I went over to feed them.

I sat on a bench to rest. A lady sitting close to me said, "Isn't it wonderful here?"

"Oh yes it is and so peaceful."

She was approaching her fifties and was dressed in a fancy jumpsuit. She was a blonde and her hair was thinning in places.

"Do you visit here a lot?" She asked.

"A couple times a year, at least I used to. I stopped for a while and this is my first time back in years."

I then realized that I had done my signature move without even being aware of it. It was just so routine vow that it was a habit.

I got up to leave and she said, "You are leaving already?"

"I have to go and get some stuff done."

"Okay, I hope to see you again."

She had sent what she wanted apparently as she was giving me all the signals and verbal cues.

I thought about it on the way home. Hmm I never thought that I would attract lesbians as well at my age, thought never crossed my mind. That would be a new experience for me as well. My husband was more adventurous that I when we were younger as he used to suggest trying a threesome and me always said no. If he were alive now and said it, I would have been way more receptive.

When I was home relaxing before bedtime, I was shocked that I kept thinking about that woman. I fantasized about my first lesbian encounter. I fell asleep thinking about her.

I kept thinking about her over the next few days and decided I would go back to the orchard. I drove there, looked around for a bit and went back to the bird sanctuary. She was nowhere in sight. I fed the birds then sat down for a bit to see if she would come along. I was just about to get up when I heard a familiar voice.

"Hello there, nice to see you again. I was hoping to see you."

She pointed to a set of townhouses not far from the orchard. They were on a hill looking down over the orchard. "I live up there. I saw when you came here and had to get dressed quickly and come over to catch you before you left."

Wow she must be loaded I thought as that was a high class neighborhood.

"Nice neighborhood," I said, "your husband and you are high earners I take it."

"That was part of my divorce settlement. The punk left me for some younger bitch. My daughter used to live with me but she is away doing work for her company."

She had spruced up a bit. Her hair was styled, she had on a touch of makeup and she was in a nice dress with matching sweater. I could see that she was staring at my legs as I'd she was waiting for something to happen. I obliged and did my routine. To my surprise she reciprocated. I was staring at her vagina. She had a strip down the middle and the rest was shaved. She glanced around and when she saw that the area was clear she pushed two fingers into her wet pussy and brought them up to her lips and licked them clean. She used her other hand to tease her clit. I was intrigued and interested.

"You can come have a look at the town house anytime. I can give you my contact info," she said.

"I have time today," I replied, *"I can look now."*

Enough was said. We both got up and she led the way.

My mind was reeling, was this really happening. I was about to have a lesbian encounter. What would I do?

When I got to the house I was still confused but felt better about it. She invited me in and led me to the living room. Her house was well kept and tastefully decorated. She fetched a nice bucket and some wine. After the third glass, I was more comfortable and receptive to whatever would happen.

She asked, "Have you ever done this before?" I shook my head indicating no. She got up and pulled me up from the couch and led me to her bedroom. There we got undressed. She took in every inch of my body. She seemed pleased enough. She was not bad herself. You could see that she went to the gym regularly and she had beautiful skin.

She sat me down on the bed and started to caress me, she started to kiss me staring with my lips and working her way done to my breasts. I was already wet from the prospect of having sex and she made me wetter. My nipples were rock hard and she moved her hand toward my pussy, she was still sucking my breasts. She started to play with my clit the she pushed her fingers in. She pulled her fingers out and sucked my juices off. I was so turned on. I was moaning uncontrollably.

She kissed me on the lips again and got up on the bed. She spread her legs and started to rub her own clit. She told me to face. Her and do the same. I watched her and she watched me. It was all extremely exciting.

"Beautiful," she purred.

We did that for a while and then she switched things up she lay down and told me to turn around and straddle her so she could eat my pussy. I did. It felt amazing. Women really know what other women want. I could play with her clit and suck it as well. She sucked up all the juice flowing from my pussy.

I started to move to her rhythm not wanting her tongue to leave my clit for a second, I was close to an orgasm, I could feel it, the sensation that was building up inside me could not be denied. I kept on sucking her pussy. I stuck my finger in and used them to thrust.

She was shaking as well. I pushed back on her tongue as the sensation heightened. I shuddered as I came. She kept on sucking. My body was weak. She somehow flipped us over and she was now the one on top. I could suck her pussy even better. She was shaking uncontrollably and she was moaning loudly. I could feel her juices running down the sides of my face. She came violently, shaking like a rag doll.

We lay beside each other spent. Never knew I could have this sort of orgasm without a dick. This was a life lesson.

"That was great; I really do hope to see you again."

"Of course you will," I said.

The moral of this story is for you to decide. I had a wonderful story to share and I shared it with you. I also enjoyed the memories that it brought back for me.

My New Boy Toy

One of my friends had told me that I should get a boy toy. What she did not know was that I had already found me a nice one. He just needed some work.

I went through a nasty divorce three years ago and finding my young man was the best thing that I have done to date.

Marcus and I are so good together. Of course there are those who feel that an older female like me should not have a guy so much younger than I as he could be happy with someone closer to his own age. I was approaching my forty second birthday and he was thirteen years younger.

He was given the choice and he decided to stay with me and trust me the relationship this far has been mutually beneficial. I will explain it all as I go on. My name is Elizabeth or Liz.

I literally am starting my life over at forty two and Marcus plays a role in that. I could actually say that he is a major part of this transition. I have the fortune of working from home. It is not that great as I tend to get bored a lot. I am a computer programmer.

My Marcus helps to quell the boredom. He lives with me and ever since some persons found that out their tongues have been wagging. When I do go out I get a lot of stares and I just let it all slide. I go out and I proudly hold hands and show my love for Marcus as I have nothing to be ashamed of. From other person point of view it is a scandal worth chatting about.

I have just surmised that they are all extremely jealous of what I have. I also assume that a lot of the women out there are extremely bored with their own lives and are just afraid to make the change and afraid of what others might say. I had to be very convincing to get him to move in the first place and as you can well imagine his mother is not happy with his choices.

Marcus is everything to me; he is my source of comfort, someone who I hold dear and of course my sex machine.

All of this did not happen immediately. It is something that I had to spend time working on, just like any relationship, compromises had to be made and differing opinions sorted. It is the effort that we both put into making it work that has made us stronger and kept the relationship going. He really has been the best thing for me, I was hurt, lonely and sex starved before I met him.

That is water under the bridge now. When we met, he was just turning twenty. I had gone out with my girls to a karaoke bar. He kept on looking at me and I had the fleeting thought that maybe, just maybe it would not be a bad idea to have a much younger man in my life for a while. He eventually came over and introduced himself, he was so cute and so shy. We started talking and eventually he wanted up and we had a great conversation despite the din of the persons singing karaoke.

Of course it would eventually come up, the question of whether or not he was involved romantically with someone. After some time he confessed that he must be strange. He felt nothing for any of the girls his age; he felt nothing for boys either.

In my own mind I was thinking that this is where my fantasy of a young stud ends as he was clearly not interested in anything sexual. I decided to give it the old try though. I could not just give up like that. He was cute, had a fantastic body from what I could see so I could only imagine what he could do when unleashed from the cage he had put himself in.

"Marcus, have a nightcap with me?"

He blushed and I convinced him that he need not be, it was fine. I would even drop him home after as he did not drive.

He mulled over the offer for a while and agreed. I also told him that I was sure I could help him discover what he really wanted sexually. I had already looked him over and his tight jeans revealed a lot. He had what he needed to do the work; it must be a serious mental block on his part. His period of celibacy or whatever he wanted to call it was about to be over.

I was extremely determined and once I had my mind set on something that I wanted, I would have it no matter what hurdles presented themselves. This would be a fun assignment for me.

I had already assumed that he may be wearing the wrong underwear and that would have to be rectified. I would have to have some serious conversations with him first though to break that mental block.

So there we were having a nightcap. I started to work my charm to see if anything would happen. I may have been forty at the time but I never stopped exercising and eating healthy so my body was in good shape. I had on a dress that had a generous split on the side so I let well-toned legs show that always helps. I also had my legs slightly apart, not enough to be vulgar, just enough to make any man wonder what was going on beyond the split.

I did not mind teasing men. It always thrilled me to see their reaction. Men don't think it but women are extremely perceptive and can read a man like a book when necessary. Flirting is just one way to know what a man thinks about you. My girlfriend Meg thinks that I ought to slow down as one day the tables could be turned and I end up in a sticky situation but it is just too much fun. I have done self-defence classes and in to pinch I should be able to defend myself.

So my flirting did not work on him as he seemed aloof to what I was doing. I was talking to him and He was responding to what I said but he had not tried to look up me dress even once. This was going to be a bit more challenging than I thought. I would have to pull out all the stops to get him out of his shell.

I started talking to him about sex and then I started to understand what the problem really was. It was psychological. He had the tools to do the job but he just was not able to get an erection. That is showy he assumed he was just not a sexual being and had stopped trying.

Meg was a psychologist by profession so I outlined his problem to her. She determined from what I said that he just needed to be loved. He ended a listening ear and someone who would not mock him about his problem but work to help solve it.

I continued to talk with him and see if I could get to the meat of the matter. I asked him if he had ever masturbated and he seemed slightly embarrassed by this question. That was it, I could use that.

He was soon ready to go home, he still lived at home and his parents would start to worry. Okay that was good to know as well. I was already trying to figure out how I would get him excited about sex next time we met. Hopefully there would be a next time. I asked him if he would like to meet with me again. He agreed. Hmm I was making progress here.

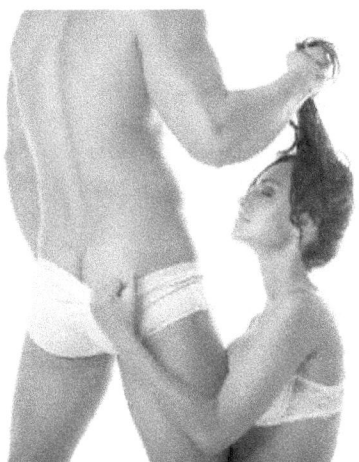

He declined my offer to drive him home and he left to go and catch the train. I gave him a kiss on the cheek and said goodbye (for now). I hoped he was not embarrassed to be seen with an older woman.

Getting him to one up became an obsession of mine. He wanted to have great, mind blowing sex to set him free, I could feel it and he need to be loved. I could give him all that and more. Of course sex is better than love. Love I something that grows over time, it cannot be forced. This had to be done cautiously, step by step. I was confident that I could do it.

About a month and a half after we met, I started to make some progress. He had come over to my house a couple times and I made sure that I had on lingerie every time.

I proudly answer the door in my underwear and act as if I was shocked that he was there. I would say I thought it was another day or a different time. The poor dear used to really be embarrassed and with head down offered to come back at another time. I would then have to drag him in saying that he was silly and that I could easily throw on a robe or something.

At least in his bold, blue eyes, I saw that spark of interest. I would let him go sit in the living room and I would go and get some refreshments including apple pie, which he had said was his favorite.

Of course I never did put on the robe. I was an incorrigible flirt and I pranced around the house in my seductive lingerie.

If I got too turned on I could always use one of my vibrators to solve my problem. I was getting bored with them though. I wanted to feel real cock in my vagina. I also missed sucking cock. I must say that I am an expert at that. That is why I was working on Marcus so hard. Of course I could always have quit and looked for someone else but I saw him as a great project, I liked him, I could tell that he had a nice sized dick and I wanted to experience that. I also loved the idea that I could teach him some new things.

I had to step up my game so on one of the visits I was there in my lingerie again. I sat beside him in all my seductive glory and kissed him.

"Marcus Bradford, I think I am in love with you," I whispered in his ear.

He smiled nervously and said that he had only ever heard that from his mother. What a mood killer. I was then thinking that he must see me as a mother figure and not as a girlfriend.

I had to do something fast to evaluate the situation. I acted as if I was drinking some iced tea and let the cup slip so it spilled all over his jeans. As you can well imagine, he jumped up trying to save the couch and had no concern for his clothing.

I told him to take the clothes off so I could wash them and dry them for him. He was concerned with what he would do while he waited.

"You can do what you like," I said coyly. I knew had he understood what I was saying. He was young but he was not dumb and I think that did it.

I gave him a robe so he could go in the bathroom and change and he looked a bit sad. I knew I had made progress; I took the clothes as he handed them to me. I caught a peek of him and as I thought he had on tight boy underwear. You know the ones mothers buy for their sons. At least I got a better look at his package. I had it all planned out, some foreplay to set the mood. It would be hard but I was up to the challenge. I would get through to him if it killed me.

This was not an opportunity to be missed. I was keen on having him experience real sexual hunger and be able to satisfy it. I would benefit and so would he.

I had not lied when I had spoken to him before. I really did love him. Meg of course thought that I loved the idea of having him a boy toy more than I loved him for who he was. I was convinced that she was jealous.

He looked fantastic in my pink robe, absolutely handsome. I informed him that his cloyed would be washed and dried soon enough. I asked him to come and sit down beside me. My heart was beating fast, I was so excited. Was this going to be the moment? It sure felt as if it would be.

I spoke to him assuring him that I was not tying him down to anything. I did love him but it was not a noose that I was tying around his neck. He was free to make his choice as to what he wanted to do in the end. He could just say what he felt and do would understand, no matter what. I also assured him that I had no concern with age.

Marcus said, "But we spoke about his and I said that I was not able to please a girl. That is not fair for you."

"Don't worry Marcus; I know what you can do for me."

I started to caress him, kissing him on the forehead. I opened my pink gown and started to rub his chest. He was a man indeed. He hugged me and that was about it from him. I started to kiss his chest, brushing his nipples and playing with his washboard stomach. I wanted to rip the gown and that damn tight underwear off but I restrained myself, looking for some sign that he was responding to my touch. Nothing... was I really trying to raise the dead here. I was not convinced.

I spoke to Meg about that experience and she was interested in having a session with him. I said no that would not be necessary, I just wanted some more pointers.

"Meg, I just want to know what to do," I said.

"You sound as if you are being possessive missy? You are not supposed to be."

"Maybe you are right; I just need to get him out of his shell."

"Well, be extremely careful, he loves his mamma and from what I have heard she is possessive and you don't want him to see you as another mother."

"Yea, I know, I know and she is almost the same age as me too come to think of it."

"Just keep on doing what you are doing, just try and exercise patience and don't get upset when he does not respond. Just do it in baby steps and keep talking to him let him know what you are doing and why you are doing it? Ask him if he likes it and ask him if he wants to return the favor."

"That is all you are giving me Meg?"

"Just be careful. He really wants to perform but don't do anything that will cause him to become even more opposed to the task."

"Don't make him feel inadequate. You can do it all if he does not want to or is unable to; you are just sharing the experience with him. Get him to spend some time in bed with you and don't wear anything. You can tell him you never wear clothes to bed and he might just oblige and do that as well."

"Some advice for you now is to just enjoy having a man beside you. That can be quite satisfying. There are women who partners who are driven by sex and would appreciate having someone who just wanted to cuddle for a change and others complain of the man with ego who thinks he must put on a big performance and he ignores the emotional part of the relationship."

"Just keep working at it. If you get him to respond it will be a victory for you. Just don't overdo things and negate the progress you have already made."

"Okay I will if you think that is the route I should take."

Meg laughed and assured me that would all be okay.

"Remember not to chastise him for not being able to perform. Oral stimulation is just as good...just let him know that you are happy."

So Marcus continued to come over on Wednesdays. That was his day off from work. I could work anytime as I worked from home so I had no problems with that. He was now excited to come over so I felt I was winning even for that interest alone.

We had snacks and iced tea as usual. He would tell me how nice I looked in what I was wearing and that it complimented my figure. He complimented me on having such a nice firm derrière.

It was a good thing in my mind. He was taking notice and he was being verbal about it. I could see that he was thrilled by certain things that I wore and certain things I did.

We would then do some light petting. He was at least having some sort of reaction now. He was very tender with me and I liked that.

I suggested that we could go and cuddle in bed and he was okay with that. I led him to my bedroom. He was noticeably nervous so I kept him calm, reminding him that we were just going to cuddle and that I expected nothing more than that. We would just be there keeping each other company.

He got out of his clothes and dived under the covers quickly. I took my time and joined him. It was great. At least he was touching me. He ran his fingers up and down my back, making me tingle and he played with my ass.

I told him I would like to kiss him and if he would mind that. He was. Okay so I kissed him. This was more passionate than the last one we had. I asked him how it was and he said he enjoyed it. I said I did as well.

I caressed him, rubbing his broad chest and just kissed and hugged. I pressed my body against his to see if I had elicited the response I wanted but there was nothing yet. I reminded myself to be patient and that there was still a lot of work to do.

After that session I spoke to my dear Meg again. We got down into the conversation about sex and she told me that a man's penis was like the staff of life.

She went on to explain that it was viewed that way because if he did not use his one is to spread his seed, we would die as a race. At least that was how it was before science came up with artificial insemination.

I wondered how this applied to my situation with Marcus. I was advised to stick to the program. It would take time and I must take the favorable responses as a sign of progress. Oral sex can always work and it would be my personal challenge to get a rise out of him. I would have done what no other woman had done before with Marcus. Once I got to that point it would be smooth sailing ahead and Marcus could always make up for all the time we spent working on his libido and his confidence.

I thanked her for her advice. She had really helped me to make progress with him.

Marcus and I continued to lie in bed together. He soon stopped diving under the covers. I kind of pitied him as he must feel a way about not having that natural sexual drive that all young hot blooded men seemed to have. I was careful not to let him know that I was thinking that of course. I just kept on encouraging him and kept on asking him before I did things and found out whether he liked it or not.

My next meeting with him would be working on getting rid of that negative energy he seemed to be carrying around about his sexuality.

The routine remained the same when he came by the following Wednesday. He was more than eager to go upstairs and he was even more comfortable getting naked in front of me. I got a good chance to really see his body and I complimented him on his physique. I expressed that I was lucky to have him and that he seemed so confident.

We kissed and hugged as usual but it was much more intense. He was caressing my back and I really liked how it felt. He took my hand and placed it on his dick.

Book 4

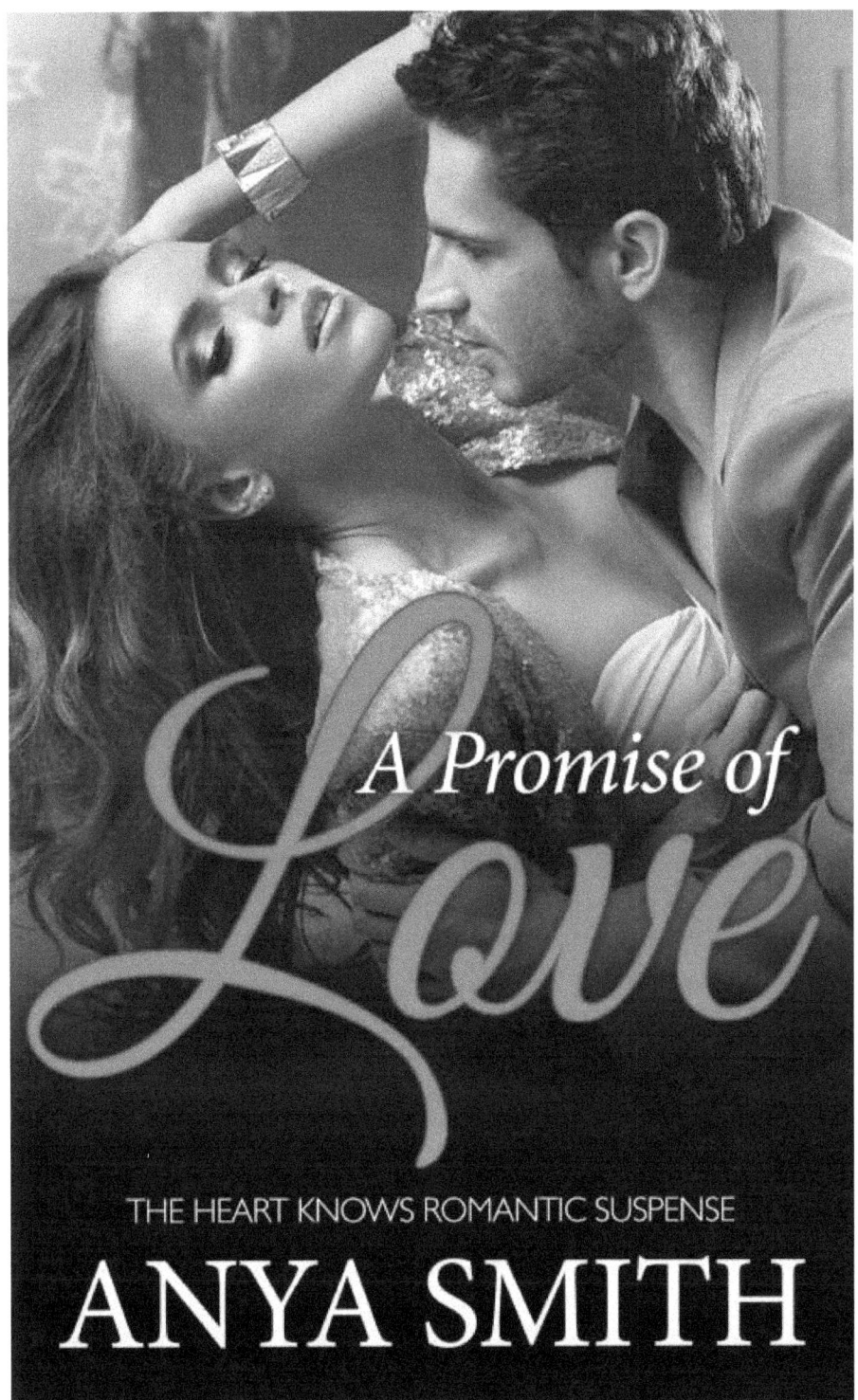

Love And Romance

"Men always want to be a woman's first love - women like to be a man's last romance."

- Oscar Wilde

The Broken Promise

It was a beautiful day in the fall and I was relaxing in the study. I was going over a contract that my secretary had just finished typing last week. As I was reading through I found an error. I did not want to come out of the study to go to my office to get a pen so I decided to look my husband's desk in the study to see if I could find a pen or a highlighter.

I found what I needed in the drawer. I glanced at his appointment calendar and could not help but smile. He had penciled in my name on Friday afternoon. I had just become a partner in my accounting firm after only twelve years and Friday was the luncheon to honor this promotion.

I continued to scan the calendar. I saw some other markings that puzzled me. Monday he had highlighted ten o clock and every Wednesday had the letter V in the afternoon. It went into the next month as well. I would ask him what those Wednesday appointments were all about. I put his pen back and headed to my office to put the contract in my briefcase. I soon forgot about the calendar as I got distracted with other matters.

I soon heard Ralph coming in. He had gone out to get our dogs back from the doggy spa. A lot of the males that lived in our community would not use their spare time for that. They would rather play golf or fish or do something else that was relaxing. Ralph was not like them. He was not born rich; he had to work hard to get to where he is today. He grew up in a household that always did their fair share of work and outside help was only gotten when it was extremely necessary. He went to wash his hands and like clockwork he went to the fridge to get a soda.

"Marilyn, I have to run to the office to complete a proposal I am working on. It should not take long and I will be back by 7pm.

He went through the door that led to the garage and I heard the garage door closing. I realized that he was out more than hang he was in nowadays. He always had something to do. Maybe I am over analyzing the situation. I tend to be home more often myself after being told I was going to be made partner. We met twenty years ago and a lot of things have happened since then.

We met at a university event. I had just completed my CPA and had just been hired by one of the leading firms in New York. I had put on my little black dress with the hope that I would make some great business contacts.

I had seen a tall lanky man standing across the room from me. He seemed to be a people person as he laughed and chatted with everyone that he encountered. He was like a magnet and I found that I could not resist walking toward him.

"Hello there, nice to meet you," he said as I approached. "My name is Ralph Mendoza and I think it is safe to say that I have not seen any woman more beautiful that you since I got here. I hope you are not offended by this and that your husband will not be offended."

He had what people would call an honest face and his smile was infectious. He hand the type of personality that made you want to stay and listen to him.

"Marilyn Johnson," I said, "newest CPA at Tanner & Feldman."

He laughed and said, "Okay Marilyn, I can see that you are all business. I am sure that I will be hearing about you in the next few years. I would love to take you out to dinner though. Is 7pm on Friday okay? It will just be good conversation accompanied by wonderful food and great wine."

I had just met him and his steel blue eyes were so captivating. I agreed to go to dinner with him. He then got his phone out to make a note of my address and phone number.

I still lived with my parents in Harrison and persons from Ralph's side of town refereed to it as one of the bourgeoisie places. A lot of persons from his neighborhood worked for the residents in my community. They either worked in a lot of the businesses that had been established by these families or worked in their homes. My father was the CEO of an events management company and he employed quite a number of persons from Ralph's neighborhood.

I attended private school with my other friends and then headed off to Harvard to get my accounting degree and then get my CPA. My dad had even set up the interview with the company that hired me.

Ralph showed up on Friday evening at 7 and I introduced him to my parents. When I got back from the date they seemed to like him even though he was not as privileged as we were. It was a nice evening. He took me to a nice Italian family owned restaurant on his side of town. They all knew him and welcomed me as if I were an old friend. The food was exquisite and they had a great selection of wine. I liked the restaurant. It was not as uptight as the restaurants that I usually went to. You could relax here.

The conversation was great as well. I gave him a little more info about myself.

"I am a CPA at Tanner & Feldman. I graduated from Harvard with honors and I am 29. I hope to be made a partner in the firm before I am 40."

"Okay Marilyn, I am 24, the fourth sibling in a family of 3 girls and 7 boys. My mother is a housekeeper and works for a family in your neighborhood and my father works in a factory. I am allergic to any sporting activity and to help my parents I started selling papers and mowing lawns when I was 10. I had to work hard to pay my way through college but I did end up getting my business degree.

He even showed me where he worked when we left the restaurant. We kept on dating and after 5 dates we had sex at his apartment which was above the office that he worked in. He was a dreamer and wanted to have a big family and give help persons from his neighborhood and other low income neighborhoods to achieve their educational goals.

The sex was absolutely crazy. We were like two sex starved animals. He was great and he could make love. Slow too. It was some of the best experiences that I have had to date. I was falling in love with him and after about 18 months, I said yes when he asked me to marry him. My parents were not in agreement with this at all. He was okay to date but not good enough to marry.

"Marilyn, please be my wife and spend the rest of your life with me. I love you and promise to support you and protect you forever."

I must admit that I was extremely surprised when he did this.

"Of course I will marry you Ralph. It is like a dream come true. I too will support you and love you unconditionally for the rest of my life."

It was a very intimate wedding so my parents did not have to make any major explanations about who I was marrying. We got married at a quaint little church in his neighborhood and his best friend was his best man and my sister was my maid of honor.

The reception was held at the church as well, in the hall. Everyone is his neighborhood came out to wish us well. My own family disappeared shortly after the ceremony was over. My father had graciously offered his beach house in Tahiti. We were like dogs in heat making love as often as we could. We did make some time to go sightseeing and to get some sun.

When we got back to the city we lived in his apartment until we had enough money to pay down on our first home. He had built his a reputation over the years which brought in more clients and I got a number of raises from my own job. Our first home was in a nice upper middle class neighborhood. I encouraged him to relocate his business but he said that he had to stay close to his clients. I even tried to show him that he could get business in our neighborhood but he was adamant that people from his neighborhood needed him more.

I was getting more clients as well as Ralph carried me to all of his business events and he made sure everyone knew that his wife was the best CPA in the tri-state area.

I did get a bit miffed when my secretary told me that a caller wanted to speak to Ralph Mendoza's wife. He was always there for me when I went home after having a bad day at work. He could always get me to believe that tomorrow would be better and that none could hold me back from what I was destined to be.

Come to think of it, he was only sad once since we had been together. It was when he heard that someone he grew up with and his children were killed in a home robbery. The wife was not at home when it happened and from what he told me, she was not coping well with what had happened which was understandable as her whole world had just caved in.

I soon got caught up with work and forgot about it. He never said any more about it anyway.

Soon Ralph started talking about having a family. He brought it up when we were having dinner on evening.

"Marilyn, we are at a comfortable place in our lives now. You are moving up in your firm and my business is doing quite well. I would love if we could start having children now as we are still young. You will still make partner before you are forty."

"Okay, give me some time to think and I will give you an answer."

He gave me the space I needed to think. We still made love every night and he did lots of new things to help his case. I relented and stopped taking the birth control pills. I had been given more responsibilities at work and I got home late but Ralph would always be waiting with a romantic dinner prepared and a great love making session afterwards.

He kept his promise and was very supportive of me. He waited for me to get home from work every night including Saturdays which I had to work to complete a job the bosses had contracted.

A Very Long Day And Night

Finally the accounts were sorted out and the job was completed. We had a celebration in the office as we were all glad it was over. This was when things started to go wrong.

I had been working alongside Barry and it the two of us who made sense out of the client's botched accounts and got everything sorted out. I was in his office having a drink with him to celebrate when he grabbed me and kissed me. He was groping me all over like a love starved beast.

We were high on our success and filled with alcohol. I never backed down from his advances but returned the favor. In no time we were both naked and he was over me fucking me hard. I was really enjoying it. We left late as we fucked three more times before calling it a night. We both showered and went our separate ways.

I never thought about what had just transpired until I was driving home. I was off the pill. I was ovulating. When I got home I had another shower and gave Ralph an excuse to not have sex with him. A few weeks later I discovered that I was pregnant. This was a problem.

Ralph was 6' 5" and he had steel blue eyes and blonde hair and he had a fair complexion; Barry on the other hand was only 5'9" and had brown eyes, black hair and was a nice chocolate complexion as he was mixed race. I was 5'7", had red hair and hazel eyes and I was rather fair.

I did not know who to turn to so I called my sister and spilled my guts. She was always there for me and could give sound advice when necessary.

"Melanie, I have a problem and I need your help. Ralph and I are working on starting a family so I am not on the pill. I was at the office a few weeks ago and we were celebrating the close of sorting out the books of a client. Things got a bit wild and I ended up having sex with one of my co-workers. I am now pregnant and I am not sure who the father is. The two men don't even look alike. How do I really handle this?"

Melanie only laughed at me and said she would call me back in a couple of days.

Barry was intentionally opting to work with me on other projects and we always ended up having sex. He was a rough one so I was always sore afterward. On the nights I had sex with him I had to make up some excuse to not have sex with Ralph.

One evening Ralph and I were at home watching a movie when the phone rang. He answered and then I saw his expression change to a somber one and he gave me the phone.

I found out it was only Melanie. "Don't worry sis, I told Ralph it was a family emergency. I have made an appointment for you at a clinic for next week Monday. They will do the abortion and then a sterilization of tubes after. It will take a couple days for you to recover so you have to refrain from having sex. You can tell Ralph I found out Edgar was cheating and that I kicked him out and I am on the verge of a nervous breakdown."

"Are you sure Melanie? Ralph can call to check up on you and what if Edgar ends up answering the phone. I do not want to create more problems."

"Oh that is sorted as well honey. Edgar is off to a director's retreat, he knows everything and he is fine with the story. He does not like Ralph anyway and still thinks you can do better."

I hung up and updated Ralph on the problem. He thought I should go and be with her and was ready to help me pack to leave in the morning. I got out of that by telling him that I had some projects that I must complete before I go. He thought that my answer was a bit strange but he simply nodded and was okay with me leaving on Saturday.

When I got to the office I told Barry I had some family issues to deal with and that we would have to work late to clear up all the projects. I also warned him to be gentle as I had to satiate my husband before I left as well.

We stayed late, worked and after everyone left we fucked. My ass was sore, my pussy was sore but he kept his word and left no tell-tale marks on my body. I was out so late that I did not get in until after midnight. I realized that Ralph no longer waited up for me. He was strangely withdrawn up to the time I left. I just shrugged it off assuming he was dealing with having me away for a couple days.

On Friday night I went home early and Ralph surprised me and took me to dinner. We did not go to his old neighborhood; instead he carried me to a rather fancy restaurant which I know he did not like.

"So did you get all the work done?"

"Yes." I found it a bit odd that he would ask me that. "Everything is sorted out. Thank you for continuing to support me, I love you even more because of this."

I reached out to hold his hand and he pulled back and said something. When I was about to ask him to repeat the waiter came with the first course and I let it pass. The rest of the evening was ok and to the topics were mostly about current events. After dinner we went home, had a nightcap and retired to bed.

When I came out of the bathroom the lights were off in the bedroom. I had neglected to put on my nightgown as I was intent on rocking his world before I left in the morning. After the procedure, it would be a while before I could have sex.

I pressed my naked body against his and he was not as enthusiastic as he usually was. He merely went through the motions and when we both came and he had recovered he carried his clothes to the bathroom.

He came out of the bathroom and went downstairs. I lay there waiting for him to come back. When I did not hear my footsteps coming up the stairs, I went to the bathroom, cleaned up, threw on my robe and went downstairs to find him.

He was sitting in the living room, he had a drink in his hand and he was just staring out the window.

"What is wrong? You are acting a bit strangely Ralph. Are you upset that I am going to go to my sisters?"

"Don't worry about it, you can a go back to bed, I just have a lot on my mind. I just need some space to sort out some issues. I need to decide how I am going to handle it."

I went back up to bed wondering why he suddenly was not sharing information with me. When I woke up in the morning, he was in the bed. I got up and started getting ready to leave. When he eventually came downstairs he was in better spirits.

There were no issues with the abortion and the pain I felt was quelled by pain pills. My sister and I had a great time reliving memories from our childhood. We spoke about old boyfriends and how they were in bed. We even laughed at the times we would have to concoct stories to get out of the house to go and spend weekend with boyfriends.

Pretty soon we got to my current situation. Melissa and Edgar really did not like Ralph and thought that I should divorce him and get more serious about Barry. He was from our neck of the woods.

I said that would not work as he was married as well and he even had kids. He was just stepping stone for me to get to my desired job in the company. As soon as I was made a junior partner I would call it quits.

When I got home on the weekend, Ralph was outside playing with the dogs. He greeted me warmly, kissing my forehead before getting my things from the trunk. He seemed to be back to normal so I assumed all was well I his world. He wanted to have sex but I told him I was under the weather.

On Monday I was back in the office. My secretary shocked me when she told me that Barry was no longer with the firm. I was flabbergasted.

"The bosses asked him to resign. He was even served divorce papers by his wife. Apparently she suspected him of cheating and hired a private detective. She never though he was really working when he stayed back late. The reason she cites in the divorce is irreconcilable differences due to him having an affair with an unknown co-worker."

I sat and listened as she continued. "The detective got pictures of him and one of our interns having sex." The bosses did their own investigation and she told them he had threatened her and said she would never make it anywhere unless she had sex with him. They advise her to file harassment charges against him and they relocated her to another office.

I was reeling. If I had not gone away last week, that could have been me in those pictures. If nothing had happened and he was still in office I would have had to make up some story as to why I could not have sex with him for two weeks.

Not even two months after that incident I was promoted to junior partner. Things were normal at home and I even got him to sell the house and get a house in a more upscale neighborhood. This is where we currently live.

I tried again to get him to move his business but he still said no as his people needed him more. Trust me, if he had not kept his promise and been supportive, I would really have left him when I started to go up the corporate ladder. He had always been there for me.

After I became junior partner, he was more accepting of me having to spend more time at the office and was okay with me working on the weekends from time to time. The only time I really saw him lose his temper was when I gave him the news that I could not have children as I was not producing eggs.

He took his time to get over it but he soon stopped trying to make love to me. I had my career and he had his business. We just lived in the same house like strangers. We were not even there at the same time anymore.

Life's Twists And Turns

It was Wednesday and it was about 12:30 as I scanned my appointment calendar. Suddenly I remembered Ralph's calendar and that I had seen the notation for V in the afternoon slot. I rushed to my car and decided to drive by his office. As I approached I slowed down to a crawl. I could see him talking to a female with brunette hair. I got a parking space on the other side of the street and start my surveillance.

They spoke for approximately forty minutes then they left his office and went across the street to a restaurant. I could not go in as I would be seen so I opted to wait in the car.

I was out there for an hour before I saw him come out of the restaurant. He was alone and he went back to his office. I don't think he saw me. I stayed there a little longer but his next visit was from an older gentleman. I decided to get back to my office.

I half expected him to say he saw me when he came home but we got through dinner and he did not say a word.

"Marilyn, for your luncheon, can I meet you in the hotel lobby or at your office. I have an appointment in the afternoon which I cannot cancel.

"You can meet me in the hotel lobby at noon. After the preambles you can slip out. That should not take more than an hour and a half. I will have to stay and mingle a bit with the partners.

As I got ready for bed that evening, I went over the last few years in my head. Ralph had not asked me to have sex with him for years, in fact not since the night I got promoted to junior partner. I was so caught up in the advancement of my career that I had ignored my marriage. Ralph had said nothing.

In that period of time I had had some one night stands and three affairs. It made me wonder what Ralph had been doing as he had an insatiable sexual appetite. He had to have had a women or women somewhere to relieve that tension. Though his business had grown over the years, he had not hired a secretary, he did everything himself.

I finished up in the bathroom and got into bed. He was already there. I moved over to him and started to caress him.

He turned away from me and said, **"Not tonight."**

I was shocked. Ever since we got married he had never passed up on having sex with me. I stayed up all night trying to figure out exactly when things went awry. I drifted off.

The alarm went off and Ralph was already up. He had made coffee and he was busy doing some work in the study. When I entered, he looked up and smiled briefly and got back to what he was doing.

I continued to get ready for work and when I was ready I realized that he was still in his robe.

"Not going into work today?" I asked.

"I just have some stuff to finish before I get dressed. I must get this paperwork done before I meet you at noon. I don't take long to get ready and I will be out of here soon."

I found his behavior strange. I went to the garage, got in my car and headed for work. When I got to work that was the furthest thing from my mind as they were all waiting for me. Everyone was clapping and smiling and one of the partners escorted me to my new plush office. I had asked keep the same secretary that had helped all of us downstairs and she was there happy for her move up as well.

I had a couple of things to sort out so I had her prepare coffee for two of us and then we sat in my office and hashed out how we would get things done from then on. Pretty soon it was time to head to the hotel for the luncheon.

As promised, Ralph was waiting for me in the lobby and he took my arm and led me to the banquet hall. I thought he was looking at three of the partners who I had slept with over the years. He gave me a curt kiss on the lips and seated me before sitting himself. As was usual with these functions, persons were busy giving congratulations with their fake smiles on.

After about 90 minutes, he kissed me again and said he had to go to his appointment.

As he walked away, I noticed that he had a certain bounce to his usual gait. He seemed relieved as if a great weight was off his shoulders. I could not shake the feeling that something was terribly wrong. The luncheon went on longer than I expected and we did not leave the hotel until after 3. I headed home and found the house empty. I lounged around waiting for Ralph to come home and when the clock struck midnight, I went to bed. I now knew how he must have felt, waiting for me all those nights.

When I woke up the next morning I could hear the neighborhood buzzing, yards were being cut and other things were being done. I had a bath and went downstairs to have some coffee. I had a quick look in the study and it seemed different. I scanned his desk and everything was neatly put away, well the supplies at least. The files he was working on and his calendar were gone.

I went back to get dressed and headed to the office. With all the hoopla about me becoming partner, I had a backlog of work. I went through it all as quickly as I could, making notations where I wanted interns to do further research. I kept on going until I heard my stomach rumbling. I packed up my files then went out to grab a light lunch.

I made a call to Ralph but got voicemail so I left a message that I was headed home.

When I got there his car was still not in the garage so I was alone at home again. I changed and sat down to watch some TV. When I was bored with that I started reading a book. I was up until 11 and I had heard nothing from Ralph. I got ready for bed. After staying up for a bit longer I decided to go to sleep. I did not want to bother his parents just yet.

I woke up and he still was not there. I ambled downstairs and had to make my own coffee. I was so used to him making it for me. I walked through the house trying to figure out how I could have thrown it all away. I was passing by Ralph's walk in close and decided to take a look inside. I jumped back in surprise when I realized that everything was gone. He had moved out and I had not even realized it.

I started to cry. I ran to the phone and dialed his cell. I go the voice mail again and I left a tear filled message begging him to come back home. I also called his office and left a message there.

I called my sister who could hardly make out wheat I was saying.

"He is gone Melissa, he is gone, he moved out and took all his things."

"Good for you sis, it is about time, he never fit in."

"But he was always there for me. He kept his promise and supported me while I pursued my dreams to be partner."

"Oh boo hoo, he has served his purpose then, grow a pair and move on," Melissa said.

I wrapped up the conversation and hung up. I was now depressed and desperate and experiencing a myriad of feelings. Calling her made me feel worse.

I threw on a pair of slacks and a shirt and drove by his office. It was closed and it was empty. Not knowing what else to do I headed to the mall and did some shopping. I returned to the empty house. I unpacked the car, prepared dinner and watched a bit of television before I went to bed.

I woke up early and made my way downstairs after having a shower and getting dressed. I made a cup of coffee and headed to the study. I could watch the sun rise from that room. I hardly noticed the beauty of it as I was just staring. There was so much that had not been said, so much that had not been done.

I had spent all my time at that firm fucking my way up the corporate ladder. What exactly had he been doing? I stayed in the study a bit longer and then headed up to get dressed for work. I finished putting on my makeup and headed out. I got to work rather early and parked in my new parking space.

I was busy checking through some accounts when the phone rang. It was an internal call. The receptionist downstairs informed me that my husband was in the lobby and if she should send him up. This as strange, he never ever came to see me at work I thought. I instructed her to do so and I sat and waited. It hit me when I hung up the phone; I was the 10 o clock appointment I had seen on his calendar.

My secretary knocked in the door and he came in. He was not smiling and his eyes were piercing blue. He had a briefcase.

"Ralph, what is going on? Where have you been and why are you here?"

He opened his briefcase, took out some papers and handed them to me.

"I am here to have you sign the divorce papers Marilyn. I want a peaceful split; all our assets will be divided equally, retirement funds being the only exception. I don't want the house or its contents, that is yours so you can just give me my half the money for that or it can be sold and the funds shared."

"Why are you doing this Ralph?" I was in shock. "Why ask for a divorce after all these years?"

"I kept my promise Marilyn. I stuck with you and supported you while you pursued your dreams. You on the other hand have not done that."

"What," I stammered. "I love and always will love you. I did not like that you did not want to move your business but that is no reason to get divorced. This can be fixed Ralph. Let's talk about it."

"You really are clueless Marilyn. Do you even remember the promise you made to me when I proposed? I kept my promise to you, you are a partner now. You never even thought about me when you opted to reach the top with devious methods. I am yet to fulfill my dream and I want the divorce so I can do that. I have signed what I need to sign already. Just get a notary in here and sign so I can get it processed."

"But I don't want a divorce. This can be worked out Ralph. We..."

"Please Marilyn, save your babbling for someone else. When you decided to fuck Barry, did you love me then? When you decided to fuck Bailey and Scott did you love me then? You fucked them Marilyn and more than once. To confirm his statements he threw down some pictures on the desk. I looked and saw myself in compromising positions with all 3 men. I was now in a heightened state of shock mixed with fear.

I looked at him and saw him as I had never seen him before. He was so sad; I could read every emotion on his face that he had kept in over the years.

"Look Marilyn, just sign the papers and let me go and fulfill my dream," he barked. "You clearly never loved me, why did you even do this?"

He produced even more documents. I looked and saw the receipts from the doctor I went to have the abortion and sterilization of tubes done. I really had no ground to stand on and when I looked at him tears were flowing freely down his cheeks.

I took the phone up and sent for the notary, called my secretary and gave him some tissues.

After the paperwork was signed by the relevant parties, I got the secretary to make two sets of copies. I kept one for myself and gave Ralph the original and a copy for himself. He got up smiled and that was it, he turned and walked out. He walked out and he seemed to be floating. He was free of a heavy burden now. I kept my end of the deal and sent him the half of the funds for the value of the house. Not even five months later, I got the divorce decree. It was over just as quickly as it all began.

And Now The End Is Near

We never crossed paths after that day in the office. When I was home on Sunday reading the paper I saw an article on him. It was a picture of him and the same woman that I had seen him with in the office that day I did my surveillance. The same lady he went to the restaurant with. There were also two children in the picture.

I read the caption. It stated that it was Ralph, his wife Cindy and their two children Stacy and Malia. I scanned the article. It was giving accolades to Ralph and his wife for all the good work they were doing for his old neighborhood through his business and her restaurant.

It was a pretty long and detailed article. They had started a non- profit company for that purpose named "Revamp Corp" and through this company they had restored quite a number of buildings in his neighborhood and they had helped so many people fulfill their educational dream. He seemed so happy in the picture, looking just like he did when I had met him all those years ago.

The next day I decided to go to the restaurant. I walked in and it was not full for lunch hour rush as yet. She saw me and called me over. She advised to sit in a booth and she came with two cups of coffee.

"Why are you here Marilyn? I know you are not here to eat."

"Well I saw the article and I had some questions about..."

"Oh the children, yes they are both for Ralph. They are fraternal twins and they will be 10 in October. I got pregnant a bit after you went to do your abortion and sterilize your tubes."

"He said all that to you," I gasped." Am I to assume you are the V in the calendar which he penciled in every Wednesday for months? He was having an affair with you?"

"Wow Marilyn, you are clueless aren't you. He was wholly and solely yours and when you made the decision to cheat on him, he would have let it slide. He was terribly hurt and his world was shattered but he was prepared to move on if you had just come clean. What really made him decide that it was over was when you sterilized your tubes. The abortion was something that he was prepared to forgive you for as well. He dedicated his whole life to you and you wrecked it mercilessly."

"When he came to me after that I decided that it was my time to ensure that I did not lose him again."

"What do you mean by again?"

"Oh, we all grew up together around here. I am the wife of his friend that died from the home robbery. I married Vincenzo but I was really in love with Ralph. Ralph had gone off to college and I decided to wait for him to come back. It was just that I was the only one who knew that."

One night after dancing and drinking, Vincenzo and I ended up having sex and I got pregnant. He asked me to get married and so we did. Ralph was even the best man at the wedding. He was hurt but he supported us through it all and never wished us any ill."

"He did let me know however that he had planned to come back for me. He did not know that I was pregnant at the time so he thought we had just fallen in love in his absence. Though he never spoke to us as he did before, we still kept in touch as good friends. No matter what are really hard to find."

She sipped her coffee. "You came into the picture a few years after. He fell head over heels in love with you and he was finally able to move on. Even though he kept his office here, we were not in contact as much as he was so busy pleasing you and supporting you a no the rest of the time he spent working hard."

When I got ill, he showed up and jumped in to help. I was still a nervous wreck from losing my husband and children to robbers. Everything had gone wrong that day. If I had not been ill, they would not have been at home as they would have gone out earlier, instead they stayed waiting for me to get back from the doctor. They were waiting to get me settled in before they went out.

"The doctors could not figure out what was wrong with me and I was incapacitated at one point. Ralph came by every day and he ensured I had my baths and meals throughout the day. I finally started to improve. He even got me to see a therapist to deal with my grief and he carried me until I could go by myself. He did everything for me. He even shopped for food and other necessities without being asked."

I sat backed not believing what I was hearing. He did all that for her and still was home for me. He really was a selfless individual. He really did care about people.

"Marilyn, he is the sort of man that once he loves you, he dedicates himself to you and you alone. He could have had a hundred naked women trying to get him to cheat on you and he would never do it because he had made a special promise to you. When you broke the promise you both made all bets were off. He never even thought of touching me until then. It is clear you never ever got to know the man you were married to.

"I did end up getting some money back from the robbery, Ralph helped me to invest it and he partnered with me to buy this building so I could fulfill my dream of having a restaurant. I had not been working after I had married Vincenzo so I needed something to get back on my feet and he helped me to do that. He even showed me how to do my accounting and how to purchase and store stock.

"Soon after you started having the affair, he found out. He was devastated and he turned to me for comfort. It was nothing sexual, he just wanted a listening ear and I gave him that. I was extremely upset as I knew you did not know what you really had. If you did, you would never have done that. He still loved you and would do anything for you; he forgave you without you even knowing it."

"He lost it when you went off to do the abortion? He figured you did it because you were not sure who you were pregnant for. He was still ready to forgive and move on. He made up his mind to stop being there for you as much when he found out about the sterilization. He lost all respect for you as you promised to try and have a family and then you went and did that. He spent so many nights crying. I just wanted to comfort him but I had to let him get over it in his own time."

"He no longer loved you and had lost all respect for you but he never left as he said he would keep his promise to you, he would stay with you until you made partner and then he would leave. I decided then and there that I would make him mine once more.

I put on my best show and he finally slept with me. I got pregnant during that period and months after had the twins. They are his and they have his name. I was okay with what those who knew had to say about me as I knew what was really going on with him.

"That is when he stopped trying to have sex with me. I was always trying to figure out why he did that. I assumed it was because he had found out about the affair."

"He may have grown up poor but he had morals that were instilled in him by his parents. He saw them work with each other and struggle to make ends meet so their children could have better and he made a promise to himself that he would do the same with whomever he married. His father never cheated and neither did his mother. They did have problems from time to time but they always found a way to resolve the issues and to continue to support each other. That was his example of who he would be as an adult and he never faltered from that until you fucked it all up."

"He was happy when you finally made partner. He was now free to leave. He just had to get through the luncheon with you and that was it. He had already started to move out his things and you were so caught up in your world that you failed to notice."

"That is why he penciled you in his calendar for Monday morning after he found out when the luncheon was. He wanted you to just sign so he could go but you were adamant that you were not divorcing. You made him relive the pain of what you did to him when he had to produce those bills and pictures of you having sex with those men. He also knew there were others but that did not matter, he had enough evidence against you."

"But I never really loved those men; it was just sex, a means to an end. I really never knew that he was aware of all that I was doing."

"Wow you really are self-absorbed aren't you? He read you wrong or the will to get to the top took over and made you into a cruel, unfeeling bitch. You were bright and capable, he knew that you would make it to the top eventually, you just opted to fast track it by sleeping with the powers that be to get a free pass. He never thought that you would stoop to that level."

"All I can say Marilyn is that I hope you are happy with your decisions and are happy in your new position. You made it. The only thing is that you do not look happy to me. Was it all really worth that sacrifice?"

With that she got up, picked up the coffee cups and went toward the kitchen.

I sat there as if in a daze. He really had known all this time and he had remained true until I did him the ultimate wrong by following the plan concocted by my sister.

Tears were running down my face. I wiped them away quickly and got up to leave before I really broke down. She had hit the nail on the head all right. I was nothing but a cold hearted bitch who was only interested in my career. I got what I was to get for my actions.

Other Books by Olive Youngly

Researching the Heart
An intriguing love story

Sylvia Williams, a young attractive heart surgeon, is driven out of her hospital by the arrogant, hateful and changeable ways of her senior research consultant, Dr Jonathan Philip-Hankle. She hates his lies and cannot trust him in any way. But when he realizes he loves her and cannot cope without her, he may have left it too late. He is researching the heart in more ways than one. How can a lovely innocent girl so cruelly treated, come to terms with an apparent conniving madman?

Denying the Heart
A Steamy Romantic Novel

Mavis, a school counsellor, stabbed by a pupil, is trying to recover when she meets a failed, hard-drinking handyman who hates the idea of love. As she feels the same way, they both deny their hearts.

The Heart Leads
An Intriguing Romantic Novel

A banker accidentally drives into a cycling nurse. He falls in love with her, but her parents insist on legal action to obtain compensation. When he leaves for a new banking position, it seems there is no hope for romance. The heart leads in strange ways.

www.ingramcontent.com/pod-product-compliance
Lightning Source LLC
Chambersburg PA
CBHW051030200725
29864CB00012B/256